THE OVENLIGHT SAGA

Baking Dough: Part 1

Stefanie Mellor

Copyright © 2023 Stefanie Mellor

All rights reserved

The characters and events portrayed in this book are fictitious. Any similarity to real persons, living or dead, is coincidental and not intended by the author. Similarity to Twilight characters is hopefully appreciated.

No part of this book may be reproduced, or stored in a retrieval system, or transmitted in any form or by any means, electronic, mechanical, photocopying, recording, or otherwise, without express written permission of the publisher.

ISBN-13: 9781234567890
ISBN-10: 1477123456

Cover design by: Aimee Williams
Library of Congress Control Number: 2018675309

- To the creator God - you deserve the credit and glory for this. To Jesus, my redeemer, my life would be very different if it wasn't for you. Thank you for giving us humans a sense of humor and the joy of laughter.

- To my favorite food in the world: pizza, and to my mom, who really told me when I was like 9 or 10 that I ate so much pizza that it was going to run through my veins.

- To my friends Cassie, Breann and Angela for telling me about this "Twilight" movie that was coming out, otherwise I would have had no idea what it was. Also, for going with me to see the 'Vampires Suck' parody movie, which really did suck and inspired me to want to write a better one.

CONTENTS

Title Page
Copyright
Dedication
Introduction
Chapter 1: The New Place ... 1
Chapter 2: The Gaze ... 11
Chapter 3: Stop Acting Like a Newborn ... 16
Chapter 4: BargainBin ... 23
Chapter 5: Valentine's Day is next Month ... 33
Chapter 6: Meet Me in the Woods ... 40
Chapter 7: The Hermit & the Little Horses ... 54
Chapter 8: Baseball with the Collins ... 66
Chapter 9: So This is My Room ... 75
Chapter 10: Blood and Chocolate ... 89
Chapter 11: The Miracle ... 103
Chapter 12: The Short Life of Mr. Fluffkins ... 120
Epilogue ... 129

| Acknowledgments | 131 |
| About The Author | 134 |

INTRODUCTION

Once upon a time, I went to see the first Twilight movie. It was "meh". Then 2 of my friends, who were Twilight superfans, invited me to go see the Twilight parody movie "Vampires Suck". It was terrible.

Growing up, my parents didn't let me see rated R movies. So, I was ill prepared for this one. For some reason, I thought it was going to be funny - which it was in a few scenes - but mostly it was...crude and vulgar and not funny (to me anyways).

After the movie was over, I remember sitting there in my theater seat - super disappointed - when the thought came to me: *"I could make a funnier parody movie than that!"*

So for the next week, that was my passion. Now, living in west Texas, this was going to be a problem, since there weren't many trees - and Twilight was filmed in the Pacific northwest. So I focused on indoor scenes and props. I knew some people who worked at a Baskin Robbins ice cream store, so that's where I got the idea of Tedwin and his family working there, and why his hands were so cold all the time. For Ella's character, I needed something the opposite of ice cream. I remembered that I had either a hat or shirt from when I worked at Papa John's Pizza, so she was going to work in a pizza place. I also remembered that when I was a kid, my mom told me I ate so much pizza that it was going to run through my veins! I thought that was a pretty cool tie-in to the whole vampire thing...and then I ran out of ideas.

I quickly forgot about the entire thing and didn't expect to think of it ever again. When I did think of it again, it was 2020 during the Covid pandemic, and I was unemployed and trying to find something productive to do.

What I realized after a few months of considering how to bring my idea to life, is that nobody can read my mind - and if I was going to be serious about this, I needed to write a script/book. But that was a scary idea! Do I read fiction? *Not much.* Have I ever written fiction? *No! (well, maybe once or twice in school, but I didn't like it.)* Have I ever written dialogue? *Nope.*

But all I could do was try. Once I started writing, ideas started flooding my brain and cracking me up! Not only had I been watching a lot of good comedy writing over the previous 5 years from *Studio C, Parks & Recreation* and *Brooklyn 9-9*, I had also seen ALL of the Twilight Saga movies **many** times, which gave me much more material to work with than the first time.

I started the writing process in January of 2021, and expected to have this entire parody written by that summer. What I didn't expect was to be diagnosed with endometrial cancer in April of that year. I was only 70% finished with writing the entire saga, so I made a promise to myself that if I survived my surgery in June, that I would publish the first 10-ish chapters as part 1, and finish part 2 at a later date, like how 'Breaking Dawn' was split into 2 movies.

Thankfully, I was able to fulfill that promise! I published part 1 in June of 2021 in a narrow window of time between my surgery and cancer treatments. Chemo, radiation and the physical and emotional side effects of all of that (plus being thrown into a post-menopausal state overnight) caused quite a delay in working on part 2. After a year and a half, I finally felt like I could start writing again. After reading over Part 1 that I had already published as an e-book, I decided to make some tweaks and add a few more funny bits to it and re-release part 1 in 2023, since I don't think it got much of a fair shot or publicity the first time around. (I am writing this now as of November 2023). I hope this will make you laugh as much as it did me!

Side note:

A majority of movie parodies and satires that I've seen go in a very crude direction, and as I've said, I don't care for that. I say, why can't stuff be funny without being dirty? So that's how I've written this. I know things don't have to be "in the gutter" to be good. So, there's no curse words or crude content.

You should also know that you don't need to have read any of the Twilight books in order to get the jokes, since this is mostly based on the Twilight movies. There are a handful of references to something Tedwin says or does in Midnight Sun (like accidentally showing his teeth to Bella or dazzling her or warning her not to fall in the ocean, and Ella doing a lot of blushing - but that's about it.) There are a few lines from other movies too (*Encino Man, Warm Bodies, Selena (with Jennifer Lopez), Wreck-It-Ralph, Home Alone, Bill & Ted's Excellent Adventure*), which are an added bonus if you get them. Happy reading!

A majority of Ella's backstory (food & clothing preferences, experiences at camp and school, etc - the rattlesnake, the bloody starburst, the incident at the mall after eating spicy burritos - and that's just in part 1) are all true and based directly on my own childhood/teenage experiences. Looking back on them, it seems that writing about them gives them another purpose - other than making my life super awkward at the time. In the first Twilight movie there's a lot of time where Bella and Edward are talking and it just plays music over that. I know they aren't talking about politics, she's only 17, so I'm sure she's just sharing weird stuff that's happened. So I substituted it with a bunch of weird stuff that's happened to me. You're welcome.

CHAPTER 1: THE NEW PLACE

Heat.
Cold.
New.
Old.

It had already been a few days since Ella was sitting on an airplane, staring down below at the bare, brown desert that slowly transformed into an endless carpet of green. She couldn't believe that she was actually living here - and not just visiting for the summer or a holiday break.

Already she was missing the pizza oven in her backyard and fresh jalapenos from her garden. She didn't think she would miss west Texas much with its dry, desert heat and blazing sky, but she wouldn't have minded just a *little bit* of warmth today.

It was cold inside her truck.

Trying to gather the nerve to go inside the high school, the previous evening's phone conversation she had with her mom, Runnawaye, swirled inside her mind.

"The first day at any school is hard - it's

get lost in a new place. You can always ask someone for help. No one's going to bite."

"Feeling lost isn't exactly a new thing for me mom," she reminded her dryly. "It's the 'talking to other people' part that I'm dreading."

Ella looked down at her watch and took a deep breath, reminding herself that she could do this, as she reflected on the countless times she had gotten turned around in the city of Odessa - the city she had lived in for the last 16 years - since her parents got divorced and her mom had moved them to Texas.

Somehow she always found her way home, but she couldn't call her mom today - this was something she would have to figure out on her own. She also reflected on the fact that her dad, Charlie, wouldn't be happy if she was tardy, not a good way to start out in a new place.

In this cold, damp town of Ports, in the state of Oregon - that she now found herself back in once again - she could never have imagined the strange world she would soon discover.

Taking another deep breath, she got out of her truck, ignoring the stares of the other kids standing near their vehicles with their friends.

She entered the school courtyard first, walking as close as she could to the wall without hitting her shoulder against the bricks.

Her boring, brown hair fell forward in a thick cascade as she stared down at the school map - successfully hiding her face - in an effort to make it to first period on time, while being as unnoticeable as possible.

A loud yell interrupted her concentration:

"PORTABELLA! *HEY!*"

As the sound reached her ears, she froze in horror. She knew the chances of someone spotting a culinary mushroom at this very moment were slim. *Someone here already knows my real name! Ugh, how can that be*???

Whipping her head to the left and to the right, she pulled strands of hair out of her eyes, trying to see how many other people might have heard - and - who this awful person was, intent on destroying her reputation as a loser before it even began.

Quickly approaching her in the breezeway was a decent looking boy with a friendly smile and an outstretched hand.

"I'm Derrick!" he proclaimed confidently, as he finally caught up and waited excitedly for her to return the handshake.

Relieved that no one else seemed to be in earshot of the exchange, but overwhelmed with an adrenaline rush of fear and dread, her hands were a little shaky, fumbling to figure out which hand to use for the handshake and which hand to hold the school map and schedule in.

Extending her right hand as she shook his, she stated as sweetly as she could muster:

"It's just Ella, okay? I really don't want anyone else to know my full name. I'm totally serious, if anybody found out, you have *no idea...*"

Derrick returned a wide smile as he interrupted her

anxious rant.

"Don't worry," he said, patting her arm, "I got your back baby."

Wanting to change the subject - as someone she just met had called her *baby* - she quickly asked, "Do you know where room 308 is?"

"Yeah, sure. I'll go with you, it's through those double doors and down the hall."

As they walked together, Ella hoped he would remember to keep his word. Even though this was high school, it didn't mean that people were going to be mature, by any means.

She was well prepared for the fact that this could be like first grade all over again, when everyone called her "porta-potty".

The first three classes of the day drudged by and it was finally time for lunch. Ella followed everyone else into the cafeteria and looked nervously around.

Derrick waved and motioned to her to come to the table he was at.

"Ella, this is Jessica Strongley and Angela Wubber, they will give you the scoop on everyone and everything - they are the eyes and ears of this place." Derrick paused and grinned at them. "No wait, I take that back - Angela and I are the eyes and ears, because we work on the newspaper, and *Jessica is the mouth*".

"Hey!" Jessica responded with a frown.

"I'm not saying it to be mean...but if anyone is going to be the mouth of the school, it's *you*."

Jess looked around. Pretty much everyone at the table was nodding slightly or had a look of polite agreement on their face.

"Well, it's not such a bad title to have" Jess said as she flipped her hair back behind her shoulder. She turned to Ella confidently, "I'm *also* the captain of the volleyball team and student council president." She went back to eating her salad and seemed okay.

"Nice to meet y'all."

Jessica wasted no time in being the mouth. "So, you're from Texas right? Do people in Texas ride horses to school?"

Ella laughed. That was a question she hadn't expected.

"It's an intriguing idea...but...no - we couldn't hurt the horses like that." The confused look on everyone's faces was priceless.

Mike finally realized Ella was kidding. "Haha, that's a good one!"

Jess chimed in with a non-enthusiastic, "That's so funny."

Angela leaned toward Ella with an excited smile. "Hey, would you mind if we put you in the feature this month in the newspaper? I'm sure a lot of people are wondering about what it's like to live in Texas. Plus, we don't get new students very often."

Ella blushed and felt flustered as she tried to think of a polite way to decline as she chewed on the end of a pen.

"Well, the part of Texas I'm from isn't very exciting - it's hot and dry and flat. The only thing really going for it is good Mexican food and sunny weather 95% of the time. You could always go for...female superhero's outfits or sensory processing disorders..."

Angela looked confused. "I don't know what the last thing you said was, you'll have to fill me in on that later...but what about female superheroes outfits? Explain."

"Well," Ella cleared her throat nervously, "it's always been funny to me that some of them wear strapless mini-dresses, like Wonder Woman and She-Ra. I mean, I can't imagine that *any* female serious about fighting crime would ever wear something like that, you know? I guess it's because men created those characters a while back...and it was their idea. I dunno, maybe ask some girls around here or some female cops or something too what they would wear. I mean, we all have those days when we just want to wear sweatpants, right?"

Ella said that jokingly, but she was not joking.

For her that day was *every single day*, and she actually wore sweatpants every day to school. When people started making fun of her for never wearing jeans, she begrudgingly bought a pair of the stiff, scratchy pants for her 7th grade, back-to-school wardrobe. The teasing thankfully stopped, but it was a constant irritation that she had to work hard to ignore.

She regretted bringing up the subject and hoped Angela would forget.

She wanted to enjoy this short span of time where

no one was teasing her. Y*et*.

She knew that eventually she *would* get teased, about so many things.

Her clumsiness and quiet nature.

Her general paleness and lack of know-how.

Driving an old clunker didn't help either.

"Hmm...actually, that's not a bad idea! Now, what was that first thing you said?"

"Um...actually, it's boring, don't waste your time, forget I said anything."

Ella turned and looked over her left shoulder to see what else there was in the cafeteria to talk about, her focus being drawn towards the back where there was a small snow cone stand with 3 people behind it - a girl and two guys.

One of them seemed like he was nice looking, but Ella couldn't tell completely because part of his head was covered in a sparkly hat.

She knew that sometimes guys can appear cute until they take their baseball caps off and they're totally bald under there or have strangely tall foreheads.

"Who are they?" she asked, still turned in their direction.

Jess obliged her request: "That's the Collins family, they moved up here from Santa Clara, California like...a few years ago. The guy you can't see very well is Jackson, and the girl with the pixie hair is Alith and they're together - like *"together" together* - and the one sitting behind the counter is Tedwin: *gorgeous, obviously* - but no one here is good enough for him. The rest are sitting at that table next to them."

She lowered her voice as she continued to explain, "but nobody ever goes over there and gets stuff from them, they're kind of...scary...and they have this way of staring at people that's super intense and creepy - like they either want to eat you or...take a bullet for you."

Ella wasn't convinced. "But it's just a snow cone, right? I mean, I can't imagine that a snow cone could taste bad. Let's go get one, my treat."

"Well you haven't seen their flavors - most of their stuff is supposed to look bloody and has gross names on purpose, like it's from a vampire movie - which I'm *obviously* not going to watch because there are no hot guys kissing anyone, just people getting bitten...and I get that it's supposed to draw, like, '*a parallel*' for blood being food or whatever, but my cousin got bitten by a vampire bat and he got rabies, so it's not funny, ok..."

Jessica droned on but Ella had stopped listening.

Derrick was right, she really was the mouth!

She continued staring at Tedwin, trying to figure out how she actually felt about the glittery hat and if his head might possibly look normal under there.

"So are you interested?" Jess asked, waiting for a response.

"Huh? Sorry. I was distracted by the sparkles over there...oh, let me guess...another kind of metaphor about vampires?"

Jessica didn't smile, she had moved on to a new

topic. "So do you need an after school job or not?"

Ella twirled her fingers together, "Huh? A job? I don't know…what kind of job?"

"Over at the BargainBin, I work in the -"

"What's a BargainBin?" Ella interrupted.

"It's like a big warehouse where you get everything in bulk and there are places to eat too. I've been promoted to evening manager at the Harrow Inn Express Cafe, and we need people for the after-school shift. Just working the register mainly. We had some people leave, so we need people to take their place."

"Oh. Why did they leave?" Ella asked curiously.

"Actually"…Jess hesitated, "I'm not sure. My boss said they quit, but that doesn't make sense to me. I think they're the hikers who went missing. There's been reports of these big black bears attacking people out in the woods…but they haven't been able to find the bears. I mean, yeah, I'm like *super worried* about them being ok and everything, but It's scary for me too. I mean, I can *totally* see myself in an FBI interview room like some lame TV show. All the police have done this entire time is put up flyers with their pictures on it - *like that's gonna help.*"

Ella went back in her mind to something Jess had previously said.

"Harrow Inn - isn't that a *pizza* place?" She asked tentatively, taking in a ragged breath, her heart galloping.

Jess sighed disappointedly, "Yeah - the only pizza place in this podunk town."

Ella couldn't believe her luck. There was *NO WAY* that Jess had actually just asked her to work at a pizza place! Surely she could not have known that pizza was her favorite food in the entire world! Plus, being an employee meant that she might get a discount.

"That's perfect!" Ella replied, unable to restrain her enthusiasm. "Of course I do - how could I not? Actually, when I was a kid, my mom told me that I ate so much pizza it was going to run through my veins!

Jessica rolled her eyes - and Ella couldn't tell if that was done jokingly or not.

"Ew, gross Ella," she said with a look of disgust. "Just be there by 4."

CHAPTER 2: THE GAZE

It was another boring day working behind the counter for Tedwin. No one ever bought a snow cone from them, even though they had some killer flavors like blood orange, tiger's blood - and Tedwin's personal favorite - black cherry & liver.

He knew people would actually like their flavors if they would just *try*...but he also understood their reasons for not coming near them.

It seemed to seep out from them - somehow - that their upbringing wasn't the same as the other high schoolers around them. Raised in various crime families and now living under Witness Protection. Violence. Bloodshed. It was so familiar.

This new existence, a new family, parents who strove for peace...would they ever get used to this and relax into it?

All this thinking made him hungry, what he really wanted to sink his teeth into right now was some fresh *sanguinaccio dolce*, but he would have to wait until tomorrow when it was his turn to work at their other location inside BargainBin that had the gelato.

Trying to make time pass, he stared blankly at the cracks in the cafeteria walls.

Alith was making Tedwin and Jackson each a cone, as they had to run the ice machines every once in a while just to make sure they were actually working.

Jackson was staring out the window - still as a statue - like he had been doing for the last 20 minutes.

No one was looking at Alith when her mind was suddenly filled with a vision. She had been carrying a cone piled high with shaved ice in each hand to give to the boys - but suddenly - both cones fell out of her hands, crashing and exploding onto the linoleum cafeteria floor.

Pieces of ice went everywhere.

Tedwin and Jackson both turned around, looking down first at the spilled ice then up at Alith's shocked face. Jackson was by her side immediately.

"What is it Alith?" they said in unison.

"Tedwin, I just saw..."

"What? What did you see?" insisted Jackson.

Alith shook her head as though she couldn't believe what she was seeing in her vision.

"Tedwin! A *girl*! A *clumsy girl* is going to come into your life!"

Tedwin looked at her endearingly. "What are you talking about, Alith ? A clumsy girl is *already* in my life."

Although he was not always so pleased with his own self-reverential cleverness, he cracked a rare smile.

Jackson quickly and angrily grabbed Tedwin's shoulder with every intention of wiping that smile right off of his face, but Alith gingerly ducked under Jackson's arm and jumped in between them, putting her face close to Jackson's.

"*Shh...shh...shhh...it's just a little...*" she repeated soothingly in Jackson's face - then turning her head to the side and scowling at Tedwin, she emphasized the words "*Not. Funny.*" She then finished her sentence intended to calm Jackson down a little as she looked him in the eyes: "*Joke.*"

This appeared to work a bit, as his hand slowly dropped from Tedwin's shoulder.

Alith stepped away, eyeing the two of them to see if Jackson was cooled off enough to behave himself. She didn't see him starting a fight the others would have to finish, so she nodded toward Tedwin that everything was ok.

Jackson took a few steps in the other direction and seemingly went back to staring out the window.

Tedwin sat back down slowly, the wooden chair creaking.

Only 10 more minutes.

He put his elbows on the counter and lay his head sideways on his folded hands.

Not gazing in any direction in particular, he realized that suddenly that gaze was being met by a girl - a girl he had never noticed before, with long brown hair and large, chocolate brown eyes - eyes that seemed too big for her small, pale face.

Tedwin was startled. He hadn't heard any new voices in the thoughts of other people that played like an ever present radio in his head. He never bothered tuning into the people she was sitting with, or anyone else at their school, their thoughts were always the same. And annoying.

Sitting up rigidly, he quickly glanced down and off to the side like he was looking for something - only to be startled again by a hard smack on the back of his head.

He immediately stood up and turned around, his hand on the back part of his head on the part that was stinging, almost colliding with Jackson, who stood close behind him with a satisfied smirk.

Now they were face to face again.

"Ow dude!" Tedwin's hand dropped to his side and his hand rolled into a fist, preparing to deliver a face punch.

"Never turn your back on your enemy," Jackson responded snarkily.

Alith was once again trying to calm the situation: "Come on guys," she said, poking her head in between them, "You don't want to make a scene."

Tedwin knew Alith was right, it was time to let this one go. He was sure that the girl had seen - how could she have not - and surely now thought of him as nothing more than a big dork.

He sighed to himself and sat back down, sideways in his chair, facing away from Alith and Jackson. With his head in his hands, he listened in to the thoughts at the girl's table, to see if he could find her voice. Nothing. Just the usual ones. And no one had seen this embarrassing incident, either.

Then thought crossed his mind: *"But...wouldn't Alith have seen?"*

He twisted around in his chair and caught her and Jackson exchanging small, secretive grins.

Alith *had, in fact*, seen Jackson get him good. But - Tedwin deserved it; plus, she liked it when Jackson protected her - even from her brother.

She couldn't tell if Ella had noticed either, but Tedwin's future had not changed.

Rosalie, however, had certainly noticed the skirmish.

She walked over to see for herself. *Ice all over the floor. Why are Alith and Jackson just standing in it, making googoo eyes at each other?*

"HELLOOO!" she stated in an annoyed tone, "Earth to Alith and Jackson! Who made this mess?"

Alith responded guiltily, "It was me."

"Clean this up. Now," Rosalie said, as she pointed at the floor with a stern face. When Escusme, their adopted mother wasn't around, Rosalie was prone to take charge of things - thinking of herself as their "mother" for all intents and purposes.

"You're not my mom," Alith stated flatly. "But fine."

CHAPTER 3: STOP ACTING LIKE A NEWBORN

When all the Collins siblings arrived home after school, Jackson and Tedwin dropped their backpacks on the floor and went off in opposite directions.

Tedwin went to search for his father and found him standing in the kitchen, poking around in their enormous, over sized fridge.

"DAD! Jackson slapped me on the back of the head when we were at school today while a girl was looking at me!"

Jackson yelled back from the upstairs hallway, "It was nothing. Stop acting like a newborn!"

Rose couldn't believe they were still fighting.

As soon as she got home, she flew up the stairs to her room and slammed the door. She was in a bad mood - again.

The cafeteria fiasco wasn't the only thing that had irritated her that day. She pulled out the carved, floral-print covered bench from underneath her mahogany vanity and mirror and plopped down.

Picking up her favorite tortoise shell brush, she began to pull it through her hair, focusing in the mirror on the part that had been bugging her all day - the part that had gotten gutter water in it.

When she and Dimmitt were going to their English class after lunch, he had tickled her side with one hand while sticking his finger in her ear with his other hand. It was while they were walking under the covered breezeway and she jumped sideways at the unexpected sensation. This was Dimmitt's way of trying to get her to lighten up, but it never worked - it only temporarily diverted her anger.

Rain was pouring off the roof in a concentrated stream from the corner of the breezeway where an aluminum downspout had become disconnected from the gutter over the weekend, and Rose's shoulder and arm momentarily interrupted the sound of the stream, making a slapping noise as it bounced off her designer-brand rain jacket.

A single lock of her golden, blonde hair had separated from the rest, sticking to her upper sleeve.

She slapped Dimmitt's chest. "You made me get my hair wet!"

"Really? Come on, babe, it's just a little water. I've never known you to have a bad hair day in your entire life."

Rose scowled at him.

Even though it was only the bottom half of a

section of her hair - technically, she didn't like it when things weren't as absolutely perfect as they could be.

Before they had the memories of their previous lives erased for their protection by the FBI, they were given the opportunity to write down general memories that they wanted to keep - given that no specific names, dates or places would be specified.

Everyone in the family had two or three things they wanted to keep a memory of, but Rose only had one. She wrote about one of the foster homes she liked being in, a fancy, two story home.

The woman stayed home with the children and the man would always give his wife a kiss first thing when he came home from work. Even from an early age, Rose knew that was what she wanted, too.

The woman had a mahogany vanity with a mirror and a bench that went underneath, covered with light pink and fuchsia floral fabric. A brush with soft, white bristles and a tortoise shell handle sat on top, and sometimes the woman used it to brush Rose's long hair and tell her beautiful fairy tales.

It wasn't the expensive furniture with its fine craftsmanship that Rose admired so much - it was part of a physical manifestation of a memory - a memory of how *perfect life could be*.

Escusme had a copy of all of her children's chosen memories in case they ever lost them, and she cherished them in her heart.

One day she came across an estate sale and

Rose's words leaped into her mind. Purchasing the mahogany set felt right, and she was glad to give it to her for her 14th birthday.

Rose had all but forgotten about that memory sheet when her parents surprised her with the set, even including a tortoise shell brush. Even though the specific memory had faded, she had to admit that it always did feel comforting to sit in front of that mirror and brush her hair, especially on a day like today.

The action of the soft bristles had replaced the matted look of the part that had gotten wet with her hair's regular volume and shine, helping her feel somewhat calmer, until she heard Jackson yell at Tedwin - stupidly calling him a newborn, then her anger flared again.

She flung the door open and stomped over to Jackson, standing in the hallway.

"Say the word Jackson: *"baby"*.

Good.

Now yell back at Tedwin to *"stop acting like a little baby"*.

Ugh, you all are so immature..." Rose muttered to herself as she stormed back to her room and slammed the door.

Alith hadn't left Jackson's side since they got home.

She smiled at him and tucked a strand of hair behind his ear, trying not to laugh. He had a harder time with grammar than the others and sometimes just said things oddly.

She could see that Tedwin wasn't going to let him live this one down, and would, in fact, tease him for *years* about it.

Tedwin was about to yell back, but pausing, he pondered if - in fact - Jackson had just called him a *newborn*!!! Oh how fun it would be to tease him about that!!!

But for now he wasn't finished with his argument.

He yelled his reply back at Jackson: "You're RIGHT - it WAS nothing! Nothing but what I've always expected: YOU not being able to take a JOKE! We're supposed to be siblings and co-workers, getting along, *REMEMBER*?

Jackson emerged from the hallway into the open loft space just above the stairs, protectively holding Alith's hand. He couldn't see Tedwin so he leaned over the railing of the stairs and loudly proclaimed his rebuttal.

"AAAND nothing compared to what it could have been: *A FULL-ON* WAR! You know how protective I feel about Alith! You hurt HER, you hurt ME!"

Tedwin stepped out of the kitchen slowly and paused before speaking, turning and looking up at Jackson and Alith.

"Don't see it that way." There was a hint of pleading in his voice.

He really did want to get along with Jackson, but he was very tempted to reply to his dumb threat of war with *"you and whose army?"* But, he knew that a snarky attitude wasn't going to help the situation.

"It was just a joke, I didn't mean her any harm," he added calmly.

Carlo was still standing there in the kitchen, patiently drinking a glass of cranberry-grape juice and still wearing his white coat from being at the animal clinic. After calmly observing the exchange, he finally he spoke in his usual, gentle manner:

"I don't want my children fighting, you're both incredibly fast and strong and you know you could hurt -"

Tedwin and Jackson looked back at each other and rolled their eyes almost immediately when Carlo started talking - they knew where the conversation was headed.

"We *know*, we *know*," Tedwin blurted out, then correcting his demeanor and stating as politely as he could, "we could hurt each other's pancreas or something like that".

He had a lot of respect and admiration for Carlo, but he wasn't in the mood for another one of his biology lectures.

Carlo smiled. Being a veterinarian had led him to see - far too many times - how a blow to the pancreas could spell disaster for a seemingly healthy creature.

He poked his head out of the kitchen so he could see both of his children's faces. "You're both taking the evening shift at the creamery for fighting at school."

Neither Jackson or Tedwin said anything, as they

were both the "suffer in silence" type.

For Jackson, it was actually more about plotting and calculating in silence - with minimal suffering.

But for Tedwin, it was actually no different than his daily grind of silence and self-loathing, a suffering with no end in sight.

"Fine. I'll just have to endure it," he muttered. He knew it was pointless to try to get out of going.

His father had the last word. "I'm sorry you feel that way - because we're leaving in 10 minutes."

CHAPTER 4: BARGAINBIN

Ella drove behind Jess's red Mustang and followed her to BargainBin after school, just to make sure she didn't get lost, since this was her first time actually going there.

It was a busy place for a small town - but there weren't a lot of places in town to get clothes or office supplies or kitchen items - especially not all in one place. Plus, there was a pizza cafe inside, so Ella knew she would be spending a lot of time in this store, whether she was working there or not.

"We have a new employee everybody!" Jess announced loudly as soon as Ella followed her behind the waist-high employee door at the end of the counter.

Mike and Derrick came out of nowhere. "Ella, hi! How's it going?" they both tried to say but awkwardly stumbled over their words in excitement.

"Great," Ella replied automatically, not thrilled about these two being her coworkers.

Jess quickly presented her with a thick black binder. "This is the employee handbook. You have to read through it before you start, company policy."

She pointed toward the red picnic tables in the food court area that were mostly empty.

"You can sit over there, and take your time. It may take you the whole shift but that's ok. We can train you on the food prep stuff tomorrow."

Ella picked an empty table and sat down. She noticed that catty-corner to Harrow Inn was another dining option, the sign said 'Cold Skin Creamery'.

Something glinted in the light - *sparkles*!

The employees were wearing the same sparkly outfits as the snow cone people at school! She stared harder.

It looked like it could possibly be some of the Collins family working there, but she didn't see the boy she had been staring at in the cafeteria.

She went back to reading the binder and after 45 minutes, she had finished. She got up and took the binder back to Jessica.

"So how much longer is the shift? I'm getting kind of hungry."

"We have about two hours left."

"Well, since I'm hungry, how about I buy one of these pizzas for my dinner and you show me how to make it."

"Yeah, we can do that, it's kinda slow anyways."

Jess showed her the basics of how to work the register and then took her back where the crusts and toppings were.

"Ah, so you only have *personal size* pizzas..." Ella muttered to herself disappointedly.

Although Ella could easily eat 6 or 7 regular sized slices of pizza, this would have to do.

Meats...cheese...veggies... Ella didn't see any jalapenos in the plastic bins.

"Is it just me, or was there no button for jalapenos in the register?

Mike, who had been silently tagging along - preoccupied with what social events he could ask Ella to - cheerfully interjected:

"Nope, but we've got these little, green, fancy pepperoncini peppers. They're Italian - just like you."

Turning to face him, Ella frowned and furrowed her eyebrows in concern. *Had Derrick told him her real name?*

"Why would you think I'm Italian?"

Mike startled and looked at her with wide eyes, like he had been caught.

"Uhh...no reason...you just...um..."

Ella sighed and changed the subject skillfully.

"Well, it just so happens that I keep a jar of jalapenos with me in my backpack. So I'm going to make myself a jalapeno and cheese pizza."

"Are you sure you don't want any sausage or pepperoni?" he said with a big smile, "Gotta get that *protein* in there for those muscles."

He playfully pinched her bicep, but Ella frowned at him again, pulling her arm away quickly.

"No. I've decided. I know what I want. Besides, I'm as healthy as a horse."

"Okay Mike, your turn to show her stuff," Jess said with her chin up, arms behind her back.

Mike dutifully showed her how to prep the crust and how much sauce and cheese to put on while Jess supervised. When he was done, Ella gleefully loaded the top with her jalapenos.

"Now this oven is where all the magic happens." He turned and grabbed a hold of the long wooden stick with a 2 pronged metal fork on the end.

"Poke the pizza a few times once it's in the oven so it doesn't get bubbles, you have to reach in through the side here. If the crust gets a bubble in it will turn into a giant bubble, and the toppings will all slide off and we will have to remake it."

Ella took the stick and gently poked the crust a few times. Mike approved.

She watched through the viewing window as the cheese turned brown and bubbly. When her baby-sized, personal pizza emerged on the other side, she stared at it in wonder.

"OOOOH! BURNED!!!" Mike blurted sarcastically, with a smile on his face.

"Beautiful," Ella said softly, as a small tear slid down her right cheek. The cheese was nice and bubbly and browned, just like she liked it.

Jess had only overheard the word "burned" while she was putting the binder back in the office, and hurried back to them, annoyed.

"Oh, that's just great. Check the temperature gauge,

Derrick probably messed with it again."

She impatiently waited while Mike went around to the other side.

"Oh Je-eess, you better come take a look at this," Mike called out.

Jess huffed as she walked over to him and Ella peered around the other side just in time to see Jess's surprised face as she witnessed what Mike was doing: some kind of dance, if you could call it that. Shaking his rear end in her general direction and doing some kind of flailing with his arms, she heard him sing in a high-pitched voice.

"*Wowm-chicka-Wowm-Wowm*".

Ella, mortified, turned around in a flash, exiting the situation as fast as she could, walking hurriedly back to the table she had been at before.

Sitting down, she shook her head to herself and exhaled a small huff - laughing a little too. If Mike's plan was to impress her or Jess with his mad dancing skills, he had *certainly failed miserably*. Although, she thought she had heard Jess's laughter as she ran off, so maybe his activity wasn't totally wasted.

She could tell Jess liked him, maybe removing herself from the situation had provided them a bonding opportunity - and an opportunity for her to see that Ella wasn't interested in him.

Ah. A lovely cheese and jalapeno pizza - just for me.

Blowing on her first slice before taking a bite, she felt someone's eyes on her. Looking up in the direction of the ice cream store, she saw the boy from before – at school – Tedwin!

Only once did her gaze meet his - it was too intense for her to look up again at him. Bashfully chewing her food, she looked down the entire time - feeling the pink creeping into her cheeks - so embarrassing.

Tedwin had been working in the walk-in freezer most of his shift, he had only come out for a minute to get a small cup of his favorite chocolate gelato. He liked the cold and the quietness, and it meant he didn't have to have any interactions with Jackson.

The smells from the pizza place nearby - the smells of food that was forbidden to them: *heated, cooked, denatured* - wafted over to their side of the warehouse.

Inside the freezer, the smell was hardly noticeable, as the cold seemed to dampen it. But Tedwin knew of a special air vent on the side of the wall in the back that no one else knew about or noticed.

If he stood near it, it was almost like a fan blowing it right in his face.

When Tedwin exited the walk-in freezer, the vent was blowing at full blast. Tedwin stopped in his tracks.

There was a new, strange smell in the air in addition to pizza.

Pickles? He thought. *No...not pickles...better than pickles.*

He had to see for himself - *smell* for himself.

He stood in the corner behind their counter - the smell was still there. He then stood over by the register where he would have a clearer view - and there was the new girl from school! Sitting at one of the tables, eating a pizza - it was *her - she must have brought this new smell.* He stared at her intently, trying to figure out what was on her pizza.

He wanted it so badly.

He couldn't read her thoughts - there was only silence when he tried. Just like in the cafeteria. This was very concerning.

Odd. Is something wrong with me? He asked himself.

He searched for someone to read.

Ah, Mike Mewton.

Not a pleasant thought, but maybe he would know.

Mike had a conversation with her about peppers - ah, a pepper! He had been frustrated and hurt that Ella had said "no" when he asked her to go to the Spring dance with him when Jess and Derrick weren't looking.

"I have to go to Tampa that weekend, non refundable ticket" she had replied apologetically, to soften his obvious disappointment.

What could be in Tampa?

Nothing mattered now - except tasting that pizza - and finding out what was in Tampa.

Ella must have felt him looking at her, because she looked up and her eyes met his. She immediately looked down again, her cheeks blushing.

Great, how am I going to do this? I can't go against my family, Tedwin thought.

He went back into the walk-in freezer to think things over.

Realizing he had forgotten his snack, he punched a bag of ice in frustration and remained there the rest of his shift.

Ella got back behind the counter when she had finished her pizza and went to find Jess.

"Hey, did you know that the Collins family are over there working at that ice cream place?"

Jess rolled her eyes. "Yeah, like I care, but don't worry about it, just ignore them like I do. Anyways, grab your stuff, it's time to leave."

Once Ella put her jar of jalapenos back in her backpack, she was ready to go.

Jess opened the door for them all and locked it behind them, then caught up with Mike and Derrick, leaving Ella walking a few steps behind them.

As they neared the exit, the shopping cart area was there in between the entrance and exit doors, and one of the carts was sticking out from the rest, it hadn't pushed back in at all, which was one of Ella's pet peeves. She wasn't in a hurry, so she figured she would just push it forward instead of walking around it. But as she tried to push it sideways and guide it forward, it seemed like it was stuck. She stepped to the side - or tried to at least, but her feet didn't want to respond. She stumbled over her left foot, watching herself fall down in slow-motion.

Then some *thing - someone* - caught her arm.

"Sorry!" she exclaimed in surprise and shame as she looked up, automatically apologizing for her clumsiness.

A face with black eyes was staring down at her.

"Can you at least watch where you're going?" the face said rudely.

She now realized that there was a hand on her upper arm that had stopped her from falling, a hand which lingered a little longer than it should have, a hand that she could feel was ice cold through her long-sleeve, plaid shirt.

Ella quickly righted herself and now that she was steady, moved the freezing hand off her arm and looked fully into the face to say thank you - *Tedwin's* face.

"I'm ok now, thanks. You're uh…Tedwin, right? I'm Ella, we go to school together…"

Tedwin's face showed no response to her question, but his black eyes had something behind them – Ella couldn't tell if it was fear or danger, but she was both curious and a little frightened at the same time.

"How did you get over to me so fast? You were nowhere near me just a second ago, I saw you all the way across the store"

"Of course I was, I was right behind you," Tedwin snapped.

Ella reeled from his tone. *Why is this guy being so rude?* "No, you were over there with your…"

Tedwin's family had now come over and stood behind Tedwin, all of them staring at Ella.

She was oddly struck for a moment at seeing them all together for the first time - their straight noses, matching golden-brown eyes and perfectly symmetrical faces - the kind that you only see in airbrushed magazine covers. The expression on each of their faces was also the same: serious, perhaps angry?

"You know what, never mind. I'm uh...I'm gonna catch up to my friends now."

"No one's going to believe you!" Tedwin called after her as she hurried away.

Jess was right, - this guy was weird. When Ella caught up to Jess, Mike and Derrick, they hadn't even noticed what had happened or that she hadn't been behind them. *I wasn't going to tell anybody* she thought to herself. Maybe if Tedwin hadn't been so rude, she would have told him that.

"Oh well, that's his fault" she muttered to herself.

Mike turned around, "Did you say something?"

"Nope, nothing."

CHAPTER 5: VALENTINE'S DAY IS NEXT MONTH

Ella was anxious. She sat down next to Angela at the lunch table because she had something important to ask her.

After putting her stuff down, she got up and went over to the salad bar, picking out some pieces of cucumber, and clumsily knocked her apple off of her plate.

A foot - or rather a shoe - stopped it from hitting the ground as it gracefully bounced into cupped hands - *Tedwin's* cupped hands.

He presented it to her as he politely greeted her with a simple "Ella": (not with a "hello" or a "hi", like a normal person).

"Thanks," she replied with a disgusted tone, "but it touched your shoe and now it's got germs all over it. You should go throw it away."

She proceeded down the salad bar line, ignoring him, in hopes that he would disappear. *Just because he saved me from falling doesn't give him an excuse to be rude to me or have some kind of claim on me.*

Tedwin was surprised - he wasn't used to people being unpleasant towards him, especially girls; his good looks pretty much guaranteed that all females were extra nice to him - regardless of their age. He followed her as she walked around to the other side of the salad bar.

Ella didn't like being followed and wasn't shy about confronting him. In fact, she had been looking forward to it, going over in her mind what she was going to say to him if - and when - he came back to school.

"Look, I appreciate you saving me the other day from falling down, but I think it would be better if we weren't friends."

Friends??? Tedwin was a bit shocked at the thought. They were barely even acquaintances.

Besides, after their strange encounter he took off - and he hadn't been at school or at work for the last week. He turned toward her and put his arm on top of the salad bar, blocking her path momentarily.

"Well, okay, before you make up your mind", he said with a friendly grin, but not large enough to show all of his teeth, "how about we hang out...like two normal people? Have fun."

"Well first, why don't you tell me why you were gone last week?"

Her response was quick and her expression was serious, not matching the light tone he was trying to set. She crossed her arms and waited to see what he would say - or if he would say anything at all.

Yeah, um, I was out of town for a few days...personal reasons."

No one at school had ever noticed when he was gone, or when he was there, really - but she did.

Tedwin didn't want to tell her that he had been sticking snow cone straws in the vent at work so he could funnel the pizza aroma into his nostrils better, and that they had run out of straws. Carlo told him it wasn't a big deal to run out - that they could just order some more from Amazon, but Tedwin told him he wanted to drive to the distribution center a few hours south of them - it would give him more time to think.

"Well, take some peanut butter popsicles with you," Carlo advised. One of the best things about Carlo was that he didn't hover, he let Tedwin have the personal time he needed - although Tedwin suspected that Carlo knew he was craving something.

After a few days of being away, he felt better able to handle the situation.

"So what's in Tampa?" Tedwin asked nonchalantly.

Ella's mouth fell open a little in surprise and she eyed him suspiciously: "How did you know about that? I only told...never mind."

Since Tedwin really hadn't answered her question, she didn't see why she had to answer his. "What do *you think* is in Tampa, Mr. know-it-all?"

"You didn't answer my question."

"Well, you haven't answered any of mine, so..."

This girl was challenging him in a way no one had before.

Hmm, what IS in Tampa? Tedwin thought.

He couldn't recall anything historically noteworthy that had happened there, or any big attractions or things like that. *Citizens of Tampa - obviously. But what were they called...?* Tedwin ushered away the first thought that came to him.

Tampanians? Tampaners? He knew they were most likely called "Tampans", but there was *no way - absolutely NO WAY* - that he was going to say any word that even remotely sounded like the word "tampon" to any girl - *no way*.

He finally gave her the only response he could conjure up: "Floridians. That's what's in Tampa."

Ella tried not to smile at his cunning response. This guy wasn't giving in easily - he was clever and smart, something most guys here definitely were not. *Maybe there was more to him than met the eye, maybe hanging out with him wouldn't be SO bad.*

"Okay, for argument's sake - let's say I agreed to hang out with you. Where would we go?"

"Well, hm. We both work at BargainBin...so...let's hang out on our break. But not where anyone could see us. We could meet in the back behind the store - it's just woods back there mostly, but there's a nice hiking trail and a bench to sit on.

It sounded nice, but Ella was unsure of why they couldn't be seen together.

"You know there's tables in the middle - why don't we just sit there? I'll bring you a pizza and you can bring me some of your ice cream."

For a normal person, it was a normal request.

Tedwin's response surprised her. "Are you kidding? If my family knew I was eating a *pizza* they would kill me and drink my blood!"

Ella wasn't sure how she felt about that statement. *It's normal for any teen to say that their parents would "kill them" for doing something*, she reasoned, *but the drinking blood part is pretty strange*.

Tedwin added reassuringly, "But I do want to try your pizza - and I mean *your* pizza, the kind you were eating the other day at one of the tables...what kind was it?" He knew what kind she was eating, but he chose to be careful about revealing anything else he had gleaned from Mike Mewton's brain.

"Cheese and jalapeno - it's the only kind I ever eat."

"Yes, you bring that, and I'll bring you something cold"

"Okay, I usually take a break at 5:30."

"Allright, see you then"

Ella took her plate of salad, and she and Tedwin each went back to their respective parts of the cafeteria.

There was only 10 minutes left of lunchtime. Ella suddenly remembered why she sat down next to Angela, the conversation with Tedwin had distracted her from her main purpose.

Angela turned and inquired about the incident with hinting eyes. "So you and Tedwin were talking over there, care to share?"

Ella could feel her cheeks starting to blush, so she

took a deep breath and laughed. "Oh, we were just talking about work stuff…"

She took a bite of her apple - one *without* nasty shoe germs on it, and got up the courage to ask while chewing slowly. "So, Angela, what's it like here at school on Valentine's Day? Like…do people have flowers and candy delivered to them in class?"

Angela shook her head and snickered, looking at Ella sympathetically. "You've been watching too many movies my dear", she said, patting her on the hand. "Plus, these are high school boys. Don't waste your time hoping for anything"

"I wasn't planning on it", Ella chuckled as she mentally breathed a big sigh of relief. "So…nothing goes on then, right? No…student council fundraisers or…secret admirer stuff?

"Nope. But it's a good thing you asked me and not Jessica," Angela mused. "Who knows what she would do with that kind of idea. Did they do something like that at your old high school?"

The bell was about to ring in a few minutes. Ella didn't want to talk about it, she wanted to be alone. "Uh…you know what? I have homework to finish. I'm going to get to English class a little early. See you there."

Ella got to the empty class room and plopped down in her chair. Crossing her arms on her desk, she laid her head down waiting for class to start. She was so relieved that at this small High School, it was looking like the day would pass unremarkably - just like any other day.

What she didn't feel like sharing with anyone was how annoying - or rather how *painful* - that day was for people like her at her old high school.

Every Valentine's Day, during first period, the members of the student council would visit classrooms - if they were holding any red carnations that meant that someone in that class was going to get one. The tradition was to sign the card from "a secret admirer", so there was always a little bit of hushed guessing and excitement around each recipient as to who sent the flower.

Ella always assumed some of the money for the flowers went towards some kind of fund or cause, but it was never publicized.

For the people who *did* receive carnations, it was a romantic and exciting day.

But for the people who didn't - and that was a lot - it was a disappointing day.

She had always wished that the deliveries could be sent to people's houses and they would open them at home - like Christmas presents, so people who didn't get anything - like her - wouldn't feel bad.

The day wasn't all bad though she remembered, as she and her Mom would usually share a heart-shaped box of chocolates and Ella would cook a special dinner. But she was ready to put that all behind her and have a fresh start.

CHAPTER 6: MEET ME IN THE WOODS

School was over.

Ella had just enough time to go home for a few minutes and get to BargainBin on time. She wondered if Tedwin was actually going to meet her on their break.

She put the pepper spray in her backpack that Charlie had given her last week, *"in case of bears"* was the reason he insisted she take it.

At 5:00 she put two pizzas in the oven: one for herself and one for Tedwin.

"I'm extra hungry today, I feel like eating two," Ella had informed Mike when he inquired what she was doing. She boxed one up and put it in her backpack, and ate the other one at her usual table.

She looked in the direction of Cold Skin Creamery, and Tedwin returned her gaze with a nod. She ate quicker than usual so she would have time to meet him.

Ella leaned over the counter and whispered towards Jess so that Mike and Derrick couldn't hear.

"Hey, I'm going for a quick walk outside for my break, be back in a few minutes." She darted out before anyone could ask why.

She walked outside and went around the building to the back.

It was nicer than she expected - it had been built right against the edge of the woods and there was a wide, gravel-paved trail in the middle. Tedwin had gone around the other side of the building so that they reached each other right where the trail started.

"Shall we?" asked Tedwin politely.

Ella eyed the trail skeptically. "Shall we what? I don't have that long on my break, certainly not enough time for a hike."

"No, no, there's a place we can sit and eat, remember?" Tedwin pointed to a log bench about 50 feet away, "If you would like to. I brought you a snow cone for you, did you bring me a pizza?"

"Yup, in my backpack."

"Good, let's go then."

It was an awkward silence as they walked to the bench, gravel crunching beneath their shoes - neither was still too sure about the other.

When they reached the log bench, they sat down and opened their backpacks.

Ella was glad the pizza box was still warm, so she took it out of her bag and opened the tabs on the top to make sure the toppings had stayed on. She used both hands to give it to Tedwin, like she was presenting him with something very special or fancy.

"One jalapeno and cheese pizza, just for you - as promised."

Tedwin stared at it for a moment before he took it. Holding it carefully in his hands, like someone would hold a newborn baby, he held it close to his face and inhaled deeply, taking the scent deep into his lungs.

"Hmmm." Tedwin's forehead furrowed and he smelled the pizza again. "No, that's not it." He closed the lid of the pizza box thoughtfully.

"*What's* not it?"

"That's not the smell I remember. It's close, but not...hmm. Can I ask you a weird question?"

Before Ella could answer, Tedwin asked if he could smell her arm.

"My arm. You want. To smell. My arm?" Ella asked incredulously.

"I just want to try something. It's more like testing a theory - for scientific purposes"

"Well...if it's for scientific purposes...I guess." Something about Tedwin's demeanor and his good grades in biology led her to trust him on this.

She pulled up her sleeve and held up her bent arm in front of him. He touched her wrist momentarily as he smelled.

"Yowch!" she flinched away from his touch automatically, "Your hands are freezing!"

"Yeah, sorry, I'm always working in the walk-in freezer - seems like they're always cold."

Suddenly, Tedwin was closer, his face inches from Ella's throat - he hadn't asked if he could smell her neck or her hair, but that's what he was doing. Ella quickly leaned back, pushing Tedwin away - her thoughts quickly jumping to the pepper spray she had in her backpack.

"*Whoa-whoa-whoa!*"

"My apologies. That was uncalled for. I just had to see. Now I'm sure."

Ella wasn't sure she wanted to ask. She straightened up, smoothing the front of her shirt. "Sure of what? I think it's time for me to leave."

"Don't go. You need to know this." Tedwin stood up and walked a few feet into the woods and stopped - leaning his hand against the trunk of one of the many tall trees that grew in Oregon like weeds grew in Texas.

No sooner than he had stopped near the tree - he was IN it: perched on one of the lower branches, peering down at Ella like a spider monkey stalking whatever it is that spider monkeys stalk.

She stared back at him - her mouth falling open as she couldn't believe his agility, his speed.

"It's you," he professed spitefully.

Ella stamped impatiently over to the tree and looked up at him, irritated and offended. "What's *me*? And why are you talking rude to me again? You know your mood swings are kind of giving me whiplash."

"Look, I thought it was the smell of the pizza. The smell of the jalapenos - but it's not. It's *you - it's your scent*. It's your smell that's been driving me crazy, that's why I had to get out of town, to get my cravings under control."

Ella froze. Under *control*??? *Cravings???* She looked wistfully back at the BargainBin building and bit her lower lip. It was only 50 feet away, plus a few more. She could make a run for it if she tried.

Tedwin knew it was time to explain before she ran away - for good.

"Here goes nothing," he thought, drawing in a deep breath.

"My family and I, we're different from other Italian...*people*. We don't eat spaghetti and meatballs and lasagna - or anything that comes out of an oven or a microwave. We call ourselves "frigitarians" because we only eat food that's refrigerated or frozen. It's sustaining, it keeps us strong and alive, but it's not fully satisfying. It wouldn't be like eating one of your pizzas for instance."

Tedwin shook his head and exhaled through his nose in an attempt to return to reality.

"But I could never do that, it would be breaking the rules. Even being around you feels dangerous for me - your scent, in your blood, it's something I could get addicted to very easily.

"Ah." Ella looked down disappointedly, "So that's it." She didn't look up as she spoke.

It was her worst fear coming true. Tedwin was just attracted to how she smelled - not *her. Now it all made sense. Why else would the cutest boy in school want to hang out with me?*

She looked up to question him and was startled to find him leaning down, close to her face. She looked so sad, and it pained him to not be able to immediately know why.

"I can't read your mind. You have to tell me what you're thinking."

"I...um...I guess...I just thought you liked me as a person. But clearly, I'm just a thing to you."

Her voice faltered, revealing how much emotion was welling up in her throat. It was unusual for her to feel so strongly in the midst of any kind of social exchange, and she tried to keep her face and mouth from contorting into the ugly-cry frown she felt coming on. "I should probably get going now."

Tedwin laughed, surprised at her response. "I tell you that my family only eats cold things - and that I think you smell amazing - and you think I don't *like* you?"

This was going to be tricky. He didn't want Ella to know just how much he admired her unique personality and an intelligence that challenged his own, but he also felt he had to reassure her just a little.

After all, Alith had seen her in her visions, and that wasn't nothing. What could he say to make her feel better? *Don't be creepy, don't be creepy*, he repeated in his head.

"I feel very...protective of you," he managed to voice hesitantly, in a lower tone than he usually spoke. "You're like my own, personal... pizza"

He winced internally, rubbing his forehead with his fingers as the words left his mouth - that also came out wrong! How come he had no problem coming back at Jackson with arguments, but when it came to Ella, his mind went fuzzy?

She had every right to be offended. He gave one last attempt to explain.

"I'm sorry, I'm sorry, I don't mean I see you as a '*thing*' or a '*pizza*' - as in objectifying you - I know you're a person, but you're a...*pizza-scented* person."

He tried to think of it in a way that Ella might understand.

"You're kind of like a Glade Plug-In or a Febreeze spray - except that you're my own personal "brand." *Yeah. My own brand.* "You smell good to me in a way that no one else does - or ever has. Is that such an offensive thing, that I think you smell nice?"

Ella should have been surprised, but at this point, she was not.

Grabbing on to one of the lower branches with her hand and stepping up about a foot or so on to a branch stump, she stopped there as she didn't want to chance climbing anything, lest Tedwin have to rescue her from falling over again. His explanation was sincere and a little bit comforting - and she didn't feel like ugly-crying anymore.

Her voice was gentler this time as she spoke. "Actually, that makes more sense than you probably realize. When I was little, my mom told me that I ate so much pizza, it was going to run through my veins."

"Wow, you really shouldn't have said that!" Tedwin said jokingly, before realizing the seriousness of what he had just said.

He shut his eyes, thinking about what might have happened to Ella if she had lived in Italy when they were there - it was such a disturbing thought that he started climbing down from the tree.

She stepped down from the branch she was standing on. They stood facing each other now, only a few feet between them. She looked perplexed, as she ought to have about that statement. "Why did you just say that?"

"Nothing. Never mind. I'll have to explain it some other time."

They stared at each other in silence - both having a vague sense that in revealing these things to each other that neither of them had actually told anyone else, a mutual vulnerability - and understanding - had been created.

Tedwin spoke first. "I'll be honest with you. I don't know if I can control myself when I'm around you. It wouldn't be appropriate for me to be walking around sniffing you all the time. But, I also know that I don't think I can stay away from you.

Her breath caught in her throat as she spoke. "Then don't."

"And trust me", he said, raising his eyebrows as he spoke, "it's not just because of the way you smell. You also have a mind like no one else I've ever met."

Emboldened by his words and the presumed

mutuality of feelings, she assured him back as she took a wobbly step closer towards him - the ground uneven and tangled with tree roots.

"I know you can control yourself," she said, steadying her arm on a branch above her head, *"You're gonna have to* - because we're going to be working at the same store and going to the same school. I can help you...or not." She shrugged. "It's up to you."

Tedwin needed some time to think things over and decide how he was going to explain things. He felt ready for their interaction to be done.

"You should go back inside. Your coworkers will be wondering where you are." His tone was curt.

"I'll go back soon, but didn't you say you brought me a snow cone?"

"Oh...right." *She had been listening.* He forgot.

Walking back to the bench and reaching down into his backpack there, he took out a styrofoam cup with a lid. "I brought you a straw too."

He handed Ella the cup and the straw. Ella sat down, putting the straw on her lap and lifted the lid off halfway to peek inside.

"What's this?" She removed the lid completely and lifted it up, showing it to him.

"Oh, no!" It didn't re-freeze like he had hoped. "I made you the snow cone at school...and I think it must have melted a little on the way to work. I stuck it in the freezer to make it cold again, but now it's just...I'm sorry, you don't have to drink that."

Ella peered down into the cup again. "No, it's okay - I mean it looks like it might taste ok...the texture might just be a little *different* than what I was expecting."

"Here" Tedwin took back the cup and the straw, "Maybe this will make it more palatable." Unwrapping the straw, he used it to punch skillfully at the small chunks of ice - and in no time - had the liquid looking much more homogenous than before. He proudly handed it back to Ella for her to see.

"Wow, how did you do that so fast?"

"Years of practice."

"Ah." Ella paused. "You didn't tell me what flavor this was."

"Oh right! Well how about you take a sip and then I'll tell you."

Ella examined the unlit, dark-red, icy depths and took a whiff. Looking up at Tedwin's grinning face she asked, "Is it cherry?"

"Yes! *Very* good! Well, *dark* cherry is one of the two ingredients."

"What's the other?"

"It's good, I promise, just try it."

Ella put the lid back on her cup and stuck the straw in it. Slowly, she drew the blood-red liquid up into her straw, still not 100% sure this wasn't some joke. When the taste reached her tongue, it was unlike anything she had ever experienced.

"It's....good!"

She chuckled at the thought of herself enjoying something that tasted so odd. Taking another sip, she closed her eyes, savoring the unique flavor.

"I'm so glad you like it. I think the black cherry balances the liver very well."

"Liver? Who came up with that...*combination*?"

"It's based off of one of our signature ice cream flavors, we figured it might also make an interesting snow cone. You know, you might like our ice creams, you should come by sometime," he offered, trying not to relay the eagerness in his voice that he felt in his heart at the idea of her being at their workplace.

Ella looked down at her watch. "Yes, well, I have to get going - you're right, Jess will start to wonder where I am. Thanks for the um...interesting treat."

She figured if she slurped it all the way back down the trail, that she would have time to throw it in the trash by the doors and no one would see her with it.

She put her backpack strap over her shoulder and noticed Tedwin's pizza still sitting on the bench. "Hey, aren't you going to eat your pizza?" she inquired.

"Yes, I have a little longer for my break. I'm just going to stay out here and eat it, enjoy the fresh air for a while."

While that was the truth, it wasn't the whole truth. He didn't want her anywhere near him when he planned to eat - but she didn't need to know about that, not now anyways. Indulging his senses, losing control - it was just too dangerous for her, as good as she smelled.

Once Ella was about 20 feet away, the crunching

noise of the gravel beneath her feet still slightly audible, he took his pizza and backpack and quickly walked further down the path, taking a barely visible side trail that only a few people could see and that only advanced hikers knew about - leading eventually to the Paiute animal reserve.

Coming upon a large tree stump, he sat down, opening the small, cardboard box once more to reveal the lovely aroma.

He considered how best to eat it. He remembered eating pizza when he was younger - by the slice. But there was no need to eat this politely, no one else was around.

He remembered seeing a pie eating contest on TV last week: no forks, not even hands - just people burying their faces in their food. This option seemed more enjoyable, more immersive.

It was time.

Warm, salty cheese. A sweet and savory tomato sauce. Bitter jalapenos, crunchy crust. It was all so magical together.

Tedwin needed to breathe. He lifted his head, gasping for air and smiling, eyes still closed. The dark vermilion of the sauce stained his lips, dripping down his chin. He wiped his mouth, looking down at his meal.

The jalapenos were creating a slow warming sensation, but not too bad, nothing he couldn't handle. He had not even tried, but had succeeded - in eating a heart-shaped hole right out of the middle.

Oh NO!

There was suddenly an intense burning pain on his tongue, spreading like fire in all directions - it felt just like a white-hot branding iron was being stuck down his throat.

LIES!!!

His internet research indicated that jalapeno peppers were a mild variety and not likely to cause much of a reaction.

He frantically rummaged through his backpack.

Ella had taken the only liquid he had.

He was a fast runner, he could probably make it back inside in 3 minutes at top speed if no one else was on the trail.

But Ella was, she wasn't back inside yet, and she was walking slow. If she saw him pass her, whether on the trail or through the vegetation - after he just said he was going to stay on his break, there was no way she would believe anything else he said.

He decided he could wait another 10 minutes until Ella was safely off the trail and back at work.

He tore off an edge of crust that didn't seem to have touched any jalapenos, it helped the burning in his throat a little. It was possible that there was a bush full of berries somewhere in a 5 minute radius. There was also a small creek in the area, but it was in the bottom of a ravine, and that was 15 minutes of hiking from where he was.

Tedwin was suddenly hit with a nauseous feeling in the pit of his stomach. He didn't know what was going on, but he didn't want to puke right there on the trail - that was something that no one needed to see.

"*You*," Tedwin said to his pizza in a raspy voice, "You're not going anywhere! You're going to be here when I get back! Okay?"

Trudging off into the brush and holding his stomach, he eventually came to a small clearing where he sat down at the base of a tree and put his head between his knees, something he had learned from Ella when she almost passed out in science class and he took her to the school nurse.

It must have been the peppers, my stomach just isn't used to foods like that.

His stomach returned to feeling better after taking a few minutes to recover by sitting very, very still. His throat was still sore from the peppers, but now enough time had passed that he could go back to work. Running didn't seem like the best idea, so he took his head out from between his knees.

Slowly standing up, he gingerly made his way back to his meal.

CHAPTER 7: THE HERMIT & THE LITTLE HORSES

Dressed in leather skins and a necklace made of seashells, a man named Laurance emerged from the brush from the eastern side of the trail only moments after Tedwin left.

His bare, calloused feet had been without the protection of shoes for many years, giving him a sense of feeling connected to the earth with every step.

He was on his daily search for anything edible he could find in the forest or its coastal waters: fish, grubs, wild mushrooms, berries and the occasional small mammal or roadkill.

He hadn't been in this part of the peninsula since last year, setting out from the more isolated areas he usually lived in to spend some time on the coast and try out the new fishing nets he had been working on.

He went down the same, nearly invisible, small trail that Tedwin had used.

Something smelled amazing.

He quickly tracked down the pizza sitting atop the tree stump. Looking closely, he could sense its warmth. Dumpster diving was not out of the question when he came near populated areas - but this was a rare prize that had been seemingly dropped right in front of him. A blessing from the Lord.

"Wow! I didn't think I would find a pizza out here...all alone...unprotected," he said out loud. He didn't expect to find anyone this far from the regular trails. Was this a trap of some kind? No, probably not.

He looked around in every direction but saw no one - and heard nothing. He could hear the voice of the pizza taunting and questioning him, asking him to justify why he had a right to it. The voices were torturous, which is why he chose to live out in the woods, away from other people and their strange looks.

Considering the heart shaped hole already eaten out of the middle, he felt a twinge of sympathy and considered doing the pizza a kindness - a kindness he usually only extended to the living, breathing things he ate.

"I'll do it quick - you won't feel a thing," he said reassuringly, gently. He knew the owner might come back at any moment. "Whoever you belong to won't be happy about my eating you...but I can't help myself, *you are so mouthwatering."*

He was bent over - not yet touching the pizza - when a low growling noise made him freeze. As he slowly stood up and turned around, coming towards him just as slowly from the edge of the brush was a strange looking creature - hairless, grayish-blue skin and a snarling mouth, full of sharp teeth.

He and the creature stood there eyeing each other for what seemed like minutes, as the creature slowly crept forward and Laurance slowly stepped backwards.

He was sure it was the smell of the pizza that had drawn it near. Was it a wolf? Perhaps a dog of some kind? A dog would have wagged its tail...but this just had a hairless tail like a rat, and it wasn't wagging.

SNAP. CRACKLE.

The sound startled Laurance - and both he and the strange creature immediately looked toward the direction it came from.

"I DON'T BELIEVE IT!" Laurance gasped.

Licking their chops, three small animals - what Laurance assumed were small horses - emerged from the dense brush.

A black one emerged first, followed by a light brown one of the same size and then a smaller, darker brown one.

The black horse took off after the strange creature, followed by the dark brown one, their hooves causing a thunderous noise despite their miniature stature. The light brown one walked in front of Laurance, eyeing him for a moment while he inhaled the aroma of the pizza.

I'll have to come back to this later, the one named Jason thought, *but for now we have to chase this intruder out of our territory*. Snorting and tossing its forelock, the little horse galloped away to join the others in pursuit of the creature.

Laurance, having no idea as to what he had just witnessed, took off as fast as his bare feet could carry him.

He continued to run down the small trail and came upon the wide, gravel trail behind BargainBin. He hesitated for a moment, looking up to see the back of the building that wasn't there last year.

He decided to take the gravel trail and run toward the building, as much as he didn't want to see anyone, it felt like a safer option for him, and a possible opportunity to warn the town folk.

After a few seconds of not hearing anything behind him, he stopped in the middle of the trail, pieces of gravel sticking to and embedding itself in his bare soles.

He turned around. Nothing.

When he turned around again he saw a girl coming toward him. Ella had lost her turquoise ring, and figured she might have dropped it somewhere on the trail.

"No, don't go that way!" Laurance shouted, waving his arms above his head. "Go back!"

Ella's jaw dropped. She had never seen this kind of person - a person dressed like they lived out in the woods - in real life - only on TV.

In spite of his odd clothing and messy hair, she called back to him, concerned for whatever he was talking about. "What's wrong? Are you okay?"

"*They're not bears* - they're...hairless dogs! And horses too, little horses! I saw them! In the woods!"

Even though Laurance didn't make it a daily practice of being around other people, he still had contact with locals across the area whom he would barter for food and supplies with, all of which were always inquiring if he had seen the mysterious bears responsible for the growing number of missing hikers.

Ella paused. *They're not bears...they're dogs?* She wasn't sure whether or not to believe him - she didn't know what kind of things he had been eating out in the woods - and the fact that he wasn't wearing any shoes didn't help his credibility.

TEDWIN! Tedwin is still out in the woods! Ella realized with a sharp gasp.

"Did you see a guy with a pizza?" she yelled back anxiously.

"I saw a pizza, but no guy. Look, you better go, tell people to stay out of these woods, we don't want anyone else getting hurt."

Ella was concerned about Tedwin. He wouldn't have left his pizza, it meant too much to him. She told Laurance they could go inside the store where they would be safe and call the police, but he freaked out.

"What? What are you *even saying right now*? No! *No!* You can't just...I can't, I can't go in there -"

She tried to calm him down. "OKAY, okay, never mind, I'll go call the police...and you..."

"I'll stay out here. I'm sorry for freaking out on you,

but people just can't say things like that to me. Ever."

"Okay. Fine." She ran back inside and called Charlie and told him about the hairless dog and the small horses.

He wasn't happy about her being out in the woods - he never was - but this wasn't just about Tedwin's safety - it was about her safety - and Charlie's. And the rest of the town too of course, but they weren't as important.

The creatures Laurance thought were little horses chased the strange intruder to the edge of their territory.

Whatever it was, they would know its scent if it tried to cross their lands again.

When they were done, the light brown one decided to go off on his own for a bit, back to the tree stump.

This horse-like creature was no regular horse -as it was, in fact, a donkey - and neither was the herd he belonged to. Spending most of their time as humans, the magic in their blood awakened when threats came near.

It had not yet been determined that the visiting chupacabra was a threat, but it was best to be on the safe side when it came to such matters.

Eating human food was usually done in human or hybrid form, but in this instance, Jason wondered what it would be like to taste human food with his equine taste buds.

Pizza isn't usually on the menu, but what could it hurt? He reasoned to himself. He wasn't much taller than the stump, so he only had to lower his muzzle a little as he began to nibble around the heart shaped hole already eaten out of the middle.

The taste was more than amazing.

Everything began to change.

He started to feel himself getting strangely lighter, as if it wasn't gravity that was holding him to the planet - but something else.

Future visions of himself eating jalapeno pizza played in his mind as though he were in a trance: he saw himself in all stages of his life, at all ages, in all kinds of restaurants, sitting down and eating pizza and sometimes picking it up; setting it down in the back seat and securing it with the seat belt so it was safe, lovingly turning around from the front seat and checking the rear view mirror to make sure it was doing okay back there; enthusiastically greeting the pizza delivery person, hugging them tightly and lifting them up and twirling them around.

He stood tall on his hindquarters, letting out a series of excited honks and screechy heehaws. Bucking his legs, he kicked in every direction in delight, then fell.

Kneeling in front of his treat - breathless - he knew he would *DO anything* - or BE *anything* - to have this snack be a part of his life. Forever.

Tilting his head up, he grabbed a corner of the box in his teeth to pull it off the stump, but was startled by the sound of a voice and let go.

"SHOOOO!! HEY!!!" Tedwin yelled, as he could

see from a distance the outline of some kind of small animal near where he had left his pizza and backpack.

He began running toward it, anxiously hoping that his pizza had not been harmed. *Probably some animal that temporarily escaped from the animal reserve*, he thought. *A wolf or a large fox perhaps, or maybe one of their pet dogs - what else would be out in the woods?. Yes, that's probably all it was, one of their pets.*

Jason swiftly turned his head and saw a human running toward him.

Keeping their existence a secret was of paramount importance. He stood to his feet and galloped away with lightning speed - widening his sturdy legs and lowering his head as he ran so that his gait and appearance would be less like a horse and more like a dog, disappearing into the forest before the human could get a good look.

Tedwin fell to his knees by the tree stump where his empty pizza box lay - torn and dirty. He delicately picked it up, cradling it in his hands.

Oh well, what's done is done. I'll just have to ask Ella to bring me another one.

"I leave you alone for 20 minutes," he said sorrowfully to the few crumbs and a small chunk of crust that remained, "and the wolves descend."

Tedwin closed the box as best he could, put his backpack on and prepared to walk back to BargainBin and finish out his shift.

He was sure that no one would have even noticed he was gone.

Alith. Great.

He wondered how much of this she had seen. No matter.

He would toss the box in the trash by the doors after he walked in, and hopefully spending time in the walk-in freezer would dampen any lingering odors.

Walking in front of Harrow Inn Pizza at a normal pace so as to not raise any suspicions about anything, he and Ella briefly exchanged glances.

Ella was relieved that Tedwin was okay.

Before he reached the employee entrance at the creamery, Alith was in his face.

"So, Tedwin, we were thinking about playing baseball on Saturday. You should ask Ella to come with us", she said perkily, standing on her tiptoes, trying to read his eyes.

It actually wasn't too bad of an idea, but his thirst was his top priority at the moment.

"Maybe. I'll see." His voice was still raspy.

Alith touched the corner of her mouth and raised her eyebrows at him. "You have something there, a little sauce…perhaps?"

Tedwin quickly wiped his mouth with the back of his hand. Alith didn't say anything else, but apparently she knew everything. She flitted away, still looking in his direction and smiling. *Could she be any more obvious? Ugh.*

He accepted the fact that it would probably be only a matter of time before his family found out about his possible friendship with the pizza-scented girl.

As for the pizza itself, he didn't know if his family could ever accept his choice.

My thirst.

Tedwin's throat burned in anticipation of something cold and wet.

He burst through the door into the employee area, sliding on knees over to the prep counter. Fine Italian marble - laid diagonally - had not just been used in the front of the store, they had used it for every square inch of the floor, even in the back - no expense had been spared.

The large, smooth tiles made them excellent for sliding, much to Tedwin's delight. Corporate had sent them two dispensers for soft, Italian ice as an upcoming summer promotional item, and one of them had been plugged in and filled with a pomegranate & raspberry flavor to do some taste testing with.

Dimmitt had shown him the best way possible to consume the frozen treat as they were leaving the evening before - after everyone else had gotten in their cars.

As soon as Tedwin's face slid under the space directly underneath the spigot, he flipped it on full blast: the reddish-purple, cold liquid pouring directly into his open mouth, down his throat.

He was almost fully satisfied and then:

PAIN.

Rose was in the freezer doing inventory when she thought she heard something. She stepped out to find Tedwin doing something absolutely disgusting and barbaric. Dimmitt she expected this from, but not Tedwin.

She slammed the top of his head and his shoulder blade with her clipboard while she yelled at him.

"NO!
WHEEZING!
The JUICE!"

Startled, he tipped over sideways and caught himself on his left hand. Spinning around swiftly, he sat down hard on the floor, slamming his back against the stainless steel, prep counter cabinet doors - shielding his face with his arms.

"Chill OUT Rose!" he cried, his voice no longer raspy, but clear and strong.

She lowered her clipboard, speaking at him angrily through clenched teeth.

"What did DAD SAY about KEEPING a LOW PROFILE!"

He threw his hands up in the air. "It doesn't matter! Nobody's going to see me back here!" He let out an exasperated sigh that ended with a disappointed growl. "Why do you hate me so much? Why can't you let me have just a little bit of fun?"

"I don't hate you," she said in a softer voice, "I don't particularly like you either." She paused and glanced down. "Look", she sighed, "I know we didn't choose this life for ourselves, or being a family. I'm sorry I lost my temper. I just...I don't want it to get messed up, you know?"

His eyes became distant as he reflected on what she said."Yeah, I know." He didn't want to mess things up either. Sometimes Rose could be tolerable.

"So, could you at least try to act human?" she asked sarcastically.

"Sure. If you could try and act human...I mean, be a little nicer, then we've got a deal." He stuck out his hand for a handshake.

Rose didn't smile, as she couldn't help but stare down at the floor. Thick, soft, crimson puddles of slush had gathered on the marble - *the imported, Italian marble* - tile floor, next to where Tedwin was sitting. The spigot wasn't completely shut off, and she felt her anger rising again as she observed the melting, sticky pools – the intense red contrasting starkly with the milky, white stone.

If that stains the floor he's SO dead.

She was over and done with being responsible for other people's messes. She didn't shake his hand in return. Instead, she waved her hand in a general sweeping motion over the whole area, then let her hand drop to her side in resignation.

"Whatever. Just...clean up after yourself."

CHAPTER 8: BASEBALL WITH THE COLLINS

The next week Tedwin stayed away from Ella, trying to figure out whether or not he should take Alith's advice and invite Ella to play baseball with his family.

Alith must have seen something, otherwise she wouldn't have said anything.

At the salad bar, Tedwin approached Ella again, trying to be nonchalant about the fact that he was there at the same time she was. He stepped closer to her while she picked through the carrot sticks.

"So, my family is going to play baseball on Saturday. You should come, if you want."

Ella looked at him with a puzzled look, her brows showing a crease in the middle.

"*Hi Tedwin, I'm doing fine, thank you for asking,*" she said sarcastically as she shoved her tray down the line.

I'm not being polite. She's frustrated with me, he

thought. "Sorry, Ella. I'm glad you are doing okay. So yeah, my family is going to play baseball and you are officially invited. You should come and hang out with me, just as friends. Have fun."

"Baseball," she cautioned, "throwing...catching. Running. Not such a good idea for me. You know how clumsy I am, are you sure you want me there?"

"Yes. I will bring my own car, we can talk afterwards if you like. I know there are some unanswered questions you still have for me."

"Well, ok - um, what time?"

"Early afternoon, probably - I'll pick you up. Just be ready by noon and you should be fine."

Ella watched Tedwin walk back to the table with his family, her eyes meeting Alith's for a brief moment, eyes that were squished up from a big smile - which she also gave to Tedwin as he walked past her chair.

Saturday was dark and cloudy as Alith predicted. Tedwin pulled up in the driveway a little before 1:00, and Ella came out before he could come to the door. When they arrived at the clearing, everyone was already in position, waiting for them.

"Family: this is Ella. Ella, this is my family."

Everyone waved politely. "That's my dad Carlo up to bat, my mom Escusme is going to be our umpire, and I think you already know who my brothers and sisters are: Jackson, Alith, Rosalie and Dimmit."

"So what do you want me to do?" Ella asked anxiously.

"We do need someone to play outfield," Escusme

offered.

Tedwin reassured her, "Don't worry, we probably won't hit any out that way anyway."

Ella looked at Tedwin blankly. *I don't even know where "outfield" is...this is so embarrassing.* "So...where should I stand?"

Tedwin guided her between 1st and 2nd base, walking beside her, his freezing hands on her upper arms - but she didn't mind as much as she did before.

"Now, walk backwards about 20 feet, and that will work." He didn't want her being close enough to the bases to think she would need to be involved, but not too far out where she felt completely unimportant.

"It's time," Alith said.

Everyone straightened up and readied themselves. She pitched a fast, smooth throw to Carlo, who cracked the ball and sent it straight in Ella's direction.

Ella froze momentarily as she watched the ball soar over her head, and followed it as Tedwin and Dimmit both jumped in the air to try reach it with their gloves, their torsos crashing together. Neither of them caught it, and they fell to the ground laughing. Dimmit was first to reach it, but by then Carlo had somehow run through all the bases, and when she turned around he had already made it to home plate.

"Here, let me have it," Tedwin said to a disappointed Dimmit, "I just want to try something." He had made a very bad decision to see if Ella could catch the ball in any capacity.

"Ella, catch."

She was already looking at him, of course, as he tossed the ball in her direction. The shocked look on Ella's face as she realized he wanted her to *catch* something was too much for him to handle and he chuckled, showing all of his teeth. Ella was too busy trying to focus on the ball to notice; it bounced off her glove, impressing Tedwin that she had even made contact.

Ella daintily picked up the ball and looked around, not knowing what to do with it.

"Throw it to Alith."

Ha. Throw it to Alith. Like it's that easy.

She put her left leg back, then stopped and looked down. *No, that doesn't feel right.* She brought her left leg even with her right leg, then put her right leg back. She was trying to remember how to stand to throw the ball, but she was getting that confused with a stance she had once learned in ballet - and to everyone else it actually did seem like she was doing some kind of strange dance.

Looking up at Alith, she thought, *Nope, I'm just going to walk it.*

She timidly walked toward Alith and stopped about 10 feet from her. Drawing her right arm back, she let the ball go and everyone's faces turned and watched as the ball flew off - not in a forward direction, but off *to the side*, gently bumping Dimmit, who had moved forward in his position - in the ankle before it rolled away on the ground.

"I'm so sorry!" Ella called out, visibly embarrassed.

"I told Tedwin not to let me play. Are you ok Dimmit?"

Dimmit chuckled. "I'm fine Ella, don't worry about it."

"Rose has an idea," Tedwin called out.

"It wasn't an *idea...*" Rose retorted loudly in an irritated voice, "it was more like a snide comment."

"What's the idea?"

"Well, if you want, you could switch places with Escusme - you don't have to throw or catch anything, just call people 'safe' or 'out' if the ball touches them before they reach the base. Does that sound better?"

"Yeah, actually that does sound better. Thank you."

Escusme smiled as she put her umpire cap on Ella and turned it around backwards. "Call them like you see them Ella," she said encouragingly. She seemed like a nice mom.

Rose was up to bat next. Ella looked momentarily back at Escusme, wondering if this was a good decision.

"They're going to try to cheat," Jackson warned her, poking his head around Rose. "Don't go for the obvious call right away, they'll be expecting that."

CRACK.

Rose hit the ball much better than Ella had expected her to. The ball sailed over Ella's head and everyone turned around to see if it was going to hit the ground or land somewhere in the trees at the edge of the clearing.

Dimmit was almost under the ball, sprinting to try

to catch up to it. He jumped in the air and turned around with a wide grin - proud of his athletic prowess - the white ball nestled safely in his glove. He threw it to Tedwin, who caught it gracefully and was intent on reaching home base before Rose to tag her out.

Rose dove into home plate, a cloud of brown dust enveloping both her and Tedwin and making both of them cough.

Oh, this is my job now, Ella thought. She scurried over to see what had actually happened, to see if Rose had made it or not. She hoped she had, she didn't think Rose liked her much and an 'out' would not make her happy.

Rose is not going to be happy.

Rose's foot was about two inches from home plate, and Tedwin held the ball in his hand, touching her calf as they both lay on the ground, panting and dirty.

"Out," Ella said matter of factly.

"That's two outs, actually - according to Italian rules," explained Dimmit, amused at seeing Rose so dirty.

Tedwin and Rose stood up at the same time - Tedwin dusted his pants off, but not Rose - she was just a little taller than Ella, and chose to show it as she stepped forward and glared down at her, face to face.

"It's just a game Rose, calm down," said Tedwin, "she's just trying to be fair and you know it."

"We'll see," Rose said sarcastically as she walked

off.

"Just ignore Rosalie, I do," assured Tedwin, "you're doing fine."

Escusme, in her gentle way, put a hand on her arm. "It's easy to tense up and hyperfocus on the ball, but don't worry about that - relax. With just a little bit of practice, I promise you'll get in the flow and perceive more of the game around you. You're doing great so far," she said with a wink and a genuine smile.

Ella followed her advice and reminded herself to relax as the game went on. Relaxing her muscles and her mind helped her immerse herself completely.

Before she knew it, she was becoming a *part* of the game - not just being an outside observer.

Time didn't exist.

The minutes slowed to micro-seconds,

Life flowed like a river around her.

Every swaying blade of grass came to a near standstill.

The song of every bird, every leaf that rushed in the tall trees - she could hear each sound individually, see every particle existing in slow-motion, there for her to take in and savor.

Ella felt more confident, more in control, more *alive* than she could ever remember feeling. The joyful emotions of belonging and community that welled up inside her were amazing - so completely and totally new.

Escusme also noticed the amazing job Ella was doing as an umpire and the change in her energy and posture.

Tedwin could hear her putting her thoughts together to compliment Ella once the game was over. *I'm so impressed with her natural umpiring abilities. I can't believe she took to it so quickly. It can take years of training and experience to get in a flow state like that. It's not something most people can control. Hmm...if it only occurs when the conditions align themselves, either the conditions just happened to be exactly right today...or this girl has super self-control.*

Tedwin was pleased that things were going so well and that Escusme had a good opinion of her so far. *Yes, it certainly does seem like conditions are aligning themselves.*

Was it too early to hope that maybe now his family would have an even number of people to play? He was even more pleased when Alith sent him a vision of future games - including a happy Ella.

"I think we're done for the day," Carlo called out.

Ella was startled as she came back to reality, feeling a little bit like she had awoken from a dream. She looked down at her watch and saw that it was already 4:30. She wobbled on her feet for a second, but quickly regained her balance. Taking a deep breath, she felt confident and strong - for the very first time in her life.

Tedwin joined her on her side of the field. "You wanna see my house before I take you back to yours? We live just a few minutes up the road." He figured she could use a few human minutes.

Ella thought for a moment. "Sure, that's fine, if it's

just for a little while."

As they turned to walk towards the car, something bright caught the corner of her eye. A beam of late afternoon sunshine had broken through the thick, heavy, grayish-blue clouds and illuminated a small spot on the field, turning the grass there into a vibrant, emerald green. Tiny drops of dew left over from the morning mist covered the ground like glittery fabric, glistening like diamonds.

Ella ran to it as quickly as she could, afraid it would disappear again behind the clouds. Turning to face the sunbeam: she closed her eyes, letting its warmth gently penetrate her arms, cheeks and forehead. As she stood in the sudden stillness, enveloped by sunlight - one singular thought seemed to cry out from every cell in her body - every fiber of her being.

> *I've never felt more alive. More...real.*
> *More myself.*
> *My time as an awkward, clumsy person was over.*
> *I was born to be an umpire.*

Ella turned around to share this exciting revelation, but found herself alone.

Everyone was already back in their vehicles, their brake lights glowing in the already fading daylight. The passenger door of Tedwin's Volvo was open and waiting for her. Briskly walking the rest of the length of the field, and wondering just how long she had stood there lost in her thoughts, she climbed in - starting a journey up a long, winding road.

CHAPTER 9: SO THIS IS MY ROOM

The silence in the car wasn't unpleasant, but Ella wanted to at least say something before they arrived at Tedwin's house.

"So has your family always played baseball?"

"Well, it IS the American past time - but it's pretty popular in Italy, too. You wouldn't think it would be, but it is."

"Italy?" she asked innocently, "Jess said y'all were from California."

Oh no. Tedwin forgot that he hadn't told Ella about that yet. It was so comfortable being with her that he felt like he could tell her anything - anything but that, not yet anyways.

"Yeah" he quickly corrected himself, "we used to live there too, but we also lived in Italy."

"Oh, that's neat," Ella replied. She suddenly remembered what she was going to ask Tedwin. "So remember when I told you that pizza ran through my veins, and you said that I shouldn't have said that? What did you mean?"

This girl is good, Tedwin thought, *she doesn't forget things. Well, here goes, I might as well tell her. If Alith has seen her as part of the family, she will find out sooner or later.*

"Okay, here goes." Tedwin took a deep breath. "So my family is actually from Sicily, which is an island just off the southern coast of Italy. No one outside of our family knows that about us, so you can't tell anyone. Things were...different there. Our last name used to be Collizzi, and we were kind of an "assistant family" to the Sicilian mafia - we weren't exactly involved in the killings, but we were involved in the red market. In America the black market is where you sell fake things like purses and watches", (he explained, in case she didn't know about that), "but in Italy the red market is where they sell human blood."

Tedwin took his eyes off the road for a moment and glanced over at Ella's face. The color had drained from her cheeks momentarily as her eyes widened at the horrific thought. She swallowed and her cheeks returned to their normal color.

"I can stop there if you want, I don't want to frighten you."

"No, I'm ok - I promise." Seeing the concern and sympathy in his amber eyes - even for just a moment - had helped her feel less afraid.

"You're sure? It's uh...complicated...and it gets worse before it gets better."

"I'm sure I can keep up," she reassured him, her curiosity overriding any and all concerns and fear. "I wanna know."

Tedwin put his focus back on the road and continued with his family's story. "Okay, this part's a little gory, so brace yourself. When the mafia puts out a *"hit"* on someone, they would be killed, that's how it works with the mafia. So where our family came in, was that we were like a clean-up crew, except we would additionally collect the blood and sell it on the red market, giving the mafia a cut, of course. Our family became pretty good at it, and over time we became known as *"La Chupa Vulturi"*, or "vulturi" for short - which in Italian means "the sucking vultures". I know it's gross, but that's what we were.

"So...what did you do with the...um...blood? Did you drink it?"

Tedwin laughed. "No, we didn't. Not exactly. We had a buyer - an anonymous source who wanted a certain kind of blood, *gourmet* blood, if you will. So, some of us became the equivalent of wine tasters - developing a literal taste for blood products on the red market, even learning how to smell or "sniff out" the kind of blood they were looking for, even while people were still alive."

Ella winced at the thought of people being walking blood-bags, but continued listening.

"I suppose that skill got passed down through the generations to some of us, me in particular. I know, it sounds gross...but it was a very profitable game. But Carlo, he didn't want to be involved in the family business anymore. He knew the blood could save lives. He wanted to help people, to put his surgical skills to a better use and go to medical school. So, we escaped. Carlo, Escusme and I. The red market was expanding to the US, and the FBI was interested in what we knew, so we told them what we knew in exchange for being in the Witness Protection Program."

Ella sat in silence for a few seconds. "So is your name ACTUALLY Tedwin then?" she chided.

"No, actually my name used to be Eduardo...but I like my new one better." She seemed to be taking this well, much better than he expected.

"Wow...that's a lot to go through," Ella murmured sympathetically, trying to get her head around all of this new and disturbing information. "So is that how you ended up here?"

"Well, the FBI relocated us first to a place in California in a city called Santa Clara, but we didn't like it there."

"Is there something wrong with that place?"

"No...not exactly, it definitely changed us all - but there were just too many vampires. So we asked if we could be relocated further north, somewhere more remote and less crowded, and that's how we ended up here.

The car slowed down as they turned into the driveway of a modern looking, 3-story home.

"Wow, is this where you live?" Ella asked incredulously.

Tedwin turned the car off and turned toward Ella. "Look, I want you to know..." Tedwin tried to find the words to say to her, hoping she hadn't been too freaked out by all the things he had just told her.

"When we go inside, I think my mom was planning on making you a pizza, but you don't have to eat it - she probably burned it since we don't cook - so don't feel pressured. I'll say '*you brought a snack and that you're not hungry, and you just would like something to drink*', ok?"

"Oh that's right..." Ella remembered that he had told her that when he brought her the cherry and liver snow cone, but a lot had happened that day and she forgot.

"So you're Italian...and you don't *cook*??" Ella snorted in laughter at the irony of the thought.

"I know, I know, it's kind of funny, right? But that's mainly Carlo's thing. When we lived in Santa Clara he went to a workshop or something as part of his medical training and learned about how heat denatures proteins and diminishes the life force - so we stick to cold or uncooked foods mainly."

Tedwin took a deep breath, surprised that all of these things he had just told her flowed out of him so easily. *Now it was her turn. What would she think?*

"So now you know about my family...freaked out yet?"

"Nope," answered Ella without even a pause, slightly opening her car door. "I'm good with weird, trust me. Shall we go inside?"

Tedwin was right about his family.

As soon as he opened the front door and let Ella go in first, the smell of burnt pizza hit them both. Not exactly "oven burned", more like microwaved for too long.

Escusme greeted them and gave Ella a hug. "We are so glad to have you in our home. We made Italiano for you, I'm sure all the baseball made you hungry."

Escusme and Rose had a conversation earlier about what to make for Ella if she came over after baseball. Tedwin had told them that her favorite food was pizza, so Escusme got a Red Baron personal microwaveable pizza at the grocery store.

Rose's contribution to the conversation was to roll her eyes and ask why Ella even needed to come over at all. Escusme didn't have special gifts like some of her children - but she did have a mother's intuition - and she knew that Ella was important.

"You've given us an excuse to use our microwave for the first time!" exclaimed Carlo as he welcomed them into their home. Dimmitt gave them a friendly wave from the kitchen with a knife in his hand and a goofy smile.

Ella's eyes widened at the sight of him with a knife - presumably splotched with tomato sauce - but Ella was a little bit unsure, given what Tedwin had just disclosed about his family's history.

"Sorry," Carlo added, I was trying to cut the pizza for you, so I let Dimmitt give a go, but it's harder than a brick!"

"It's ok, she already ate," said Tedwin, looking at Ella and winking.

"How about a cold one, Ella?" Dimmitt called out toward her.

Ella stared at both Carlo and Dimmitt in disbelief. "Uh, a *cold one?*" she stammered, "what are you...I can't even...no! No way! you know my dad is a cop -" Carlo put his hand up and interrupted her with a kind smile.

"It's a Collizzi...I mean a *Collins'* family joke," Carlo said as he chuckled. "We would never ask the daughter of our very own police chief to engage in underage drinking, would we family? I'm sure Tedwin explained our special diet to you already, did he not?

"Yes, he did," Ella said as she exhaled a sigh of relief, managing to smile shyly.

All the members of Tedwin's family - except for Rose - burst into friendly laughter. In her opinion, this girl had not earned any right to know anything about their family and no one else seemed to share her concern.

Carlo was standing in front of the family's enormous refrigerator. He opened the door, revealing a plethora of juices and drinks, in a variety of red and purple shades and hues. "What would you like, Ella?"

His voice echoed a little while he popped his head inside, calling out their inventory. "We've got all kinds of things in here: Red Bull, Big Red, V8, watermelon Kool-Aid, cranberry juice, grape juice, pomegranate juice, dark cherry juice - what are you in the mood for?

"Um, I'll just have a water, thanks."

"How about a tour of the rest of the house?" Tedwin

asked already halfway up the stairs, looking down at Ella.

"Sure." She held onto the super-cold bottled water that Carlo had given her and followed Tedwin up the stairs into a bright, rectangular room, full of windows.

"So, this is my room," he stated as he turned around, looking down humbly and moving out of the doorway so she could come in.

"It's so light and open in here...I like it, it's nice."

"Is it what you were expecting?"

"Hmm...I don't know what I was expecting," Ella confessed as she turned and looked at his rows of shelves. "Wow, you have so many stuffed animals! I definitely was not expecting that!"

Tedwin walked over to his collection and pointed out some of his favorites. "Bugs Bunny...Porky Pig...Daffy Duck." He realized Ella might not even know who these characters were, as they were from an older cartoon, but it was worth a shot.

Eyeing Tedwin head to toe, she paused before answering - wanting to make him squirm just a bit as he waited to see how she would respond - *serves him right for trying to make me catch a ball*!

"*Looney Toons* is great." [this is a reference to *"Clair de Lune* is great" that I want the reader to enjoy, and had to point out]

Tedwin paused as he felt a strange feeling of joy come over him in this small thing they had in common. "It's how I learned English!" he exclaimed - his upper lip curling over his teeth in a full smile this time - making no effort to hide it.

Ella held out her hand for Bugs Bunny and Tedwin happily handed it to her. She rubbed its fuzzy ears and over sized, white feet.

"You know sometimes I have...I wake up in the middle of the night, and I can't go back to sleep...so I go downstairs and watch TV for a while. Cartoon Network has been showing episodes all night lately. As silly as it sounds, those cartoons help take my mind off of my fear of being abandoned in the middle of the woods over and over and over again."

"Wow. So that's what you dream about...being abandoned in the woods?"

"Yeah, sometimes - but I also sometimes dream that there's someone in my room watching me sleep." She laughed to herself, surprised she had revealed something so personal. "It's weird."

Tedwin quickly pointed out his other collection further down the shelf to change the topic of conversation. "I have most of the characters from *Sesame Street* too: Burt, Ernie, Snuffleupagus, Big Bird..."

"No way! You have my favorite! May I?" Ella reached over and picked up The Count - the vampire character that helped kids learn their numbers.

Tedwin was surprised. He thought her favorite would have been something cute and cuddly, not a bloodsucking demon - but *oh well, to each his own*, he mused.

"Of course - why is he your favorite?" He asked curiously.

"Wow! This one is so heavy," she exclaimed, "I've never seen a *Sesame Street* doll before!"

"Yeah, that one was made special - it's Italian porcelain. Heavy and cold - but very rare as far as I know, I think they only made a few."

Ella ran her fingers over the smooth, cool surface. "Even though I knew he was supposed to be kind of *"scary"*, I always knew it was just a mask - deep down he really loved helping kids learn how to count, it made him happy. Actually...he was the one who taught ME how to count. Aw look, they even carved his little cape."

Ella was going to ask Tedwin something but she was momentarily distracted by his smile.

She looked away so she could gather her thoughts. "So, how old were you when you learned English?"

"Uh, I think I was about 6 or 7." Tedwin sat down on the edge of his couch and folded his hands, interlocking his fingers together. "I was about 10 when Carlo decided he wanted us to leave." His mood darkened, serious thoughts once again entered his mind - remorse and sadness stirred in his stomach, causing him to emit a sigh, louder than he intended to - unable to disguise the pained look on his face.

"What is it?"

"So...you need to know something about me. It wasn't just Carlo that was involved in the crimes," he confessed. "I was there too. I saw things...and participated sometimes, too. I would usually go with them on the job because they told me it looked less suspicious to have a child in the car with them, in case they got stopped by the police. You asked why you shouldn't have told me that pizza ran through your veins? Well, it's because in that moment I remembered what would have happened to you if we - or I - had come across you in Italy. The way your blood smells - it would have ended badly for you. It reminded me of who I am - of all that bad things I've done. Listen...I'm a bad guy, Ella"

"No, you're not, I can tell that you're not. It's ok. You were just a child."

Tedwin looked down at his folded hands. Ella sat down beside him, holding the doll on her lap.

"I can see that Carlo isn't the only reason you don't kill people," she said gently, placing one of her hands on top of his.

Tedwin was silent. Inside he was freaking out a little because a girl was touching him, but he didn't want her to know that, so he sat still for a moment before he spoke.

"Yeah...you're right.

He's *not* the only reason.

I don't...

want to be...

a MOBSTER."

He looked at Ella sitting beside him - deep into her chocolate eyes - and suddenly felt very afraid of making those eyes go away, of being away *from* them. Then the fear of what he had just divulged in her presence struck him with full force.

"Look Ella you can't tell anyone because if you do

- even Charlie, I know he's a cop - but you can't tell Charlie - or anyone - because if *anyone* finds out...we will have to disappear and it'll be like...like we never existed."

"I wasn't going to tell...anyone," she reassured, "I'm glad you told me the truth. I'm not scared of your "crime mob family", or any of that. I'm only scared of making you go away."

They stared at each other for a moment - Ella felt her cheeks flushing as she looked down, embarrassed that she had given away her emotions. Admitting that she wanted Tedwin to stay - actually saying it out loud - jarred her.

"Well," Ella stated, as she stood up and extended her arms holding The Count doll towards Tedwin. "I should probably be getting home now. Thanks for letting me see your stuff."

A lot of things had been shared and she needed some alone time to process it all and figure out how she felt about it.

"No, you keep him."

"Wow, are you sure?"

"Yeah...in case you can't sleep. Maybe he can remind you to count sheep. You know, because he likes to count."

Ella took the doll and they got back in Tedwin's Volvo. As Ella was reaching for her seat belt, she momentarily glanced back up at Tedwin's house - and for a brief moment - she could have sworn that she saw all the faces of his family, pressed up against the windows, watching them. Ella blinked and suddenly they were all gone.

The ride back to Ella's house was mostly silent. Not an awkward silence, a comfortable silence. Each of them were thinking about the events of the day and were content to not ask any more questions of each other - at least not for today.

As Tedwin pulled into her driveway, he didn't want to just tell her goodbye, he wanted to let her know how impressed he was with her umpiring skills - but without embarrassing her.

He was aware that he needed to use a friendly tone, but not the tone he used on so many other females, where his voice was as smooth and warm as melted butter. *Think about Alith, like you're just talking to Alith*.

"So, listen, you really did great for your first time as an umpire. You seemed like you were really in "the zone", you know? You watched the game and made fair calls - even mature umpires have problems with that."

Ella didn't disagree with what he said, nor did she feel embarrassed at his compliment. She unbuckled her seat belt and then turned to look at him to thank him and tell him about the revelation she had, but she stared into his amber, brown eyes for a second too long and forgot what she was going to say. Her face flushed pink and she turned away, trying to hide behind her hair.

Now she was embarrassed. She had let Tedwin dazzle her - *again*. She quickly cradled *The Count* doll against her as she pulled the door latch open with her other hand.

"I'll...see you later," she mumbled, ducking the gaze that followed her to her front door.

Ugh, I'm so stupid. Why do I let him get to me like that? I didn't even thank him. I'm such a...ugh.

Tedwin laughed in a way he hadn't laughed in a long time.

Not only was it funny to watch Ella stomping off holding a doll, but she was muttering, which allowed him a rare insight into her mind that was usually guarded by a wall of silence. What she didn't know was that she had dazzled him too - which she didn't believe was possible with her ordinary, brown eyes.

He was completely tongue tied - and his usually sharp mind was just a blob of nothingness - all he could do was watch and smile as she marched to her front door and slipped inside.

CHAPTER 10: BLOOD AND CHOCOLATE

It's a good day for ice cream, oddly sunny for a February day,
Ella thought as she tossed her backpack into her truck, shoving it over as she sat down.

She hadn't yet gone over to see where Tedwin worked - she was going to ask him in class, but strangely none of the Collins family were in school that day. She hoped that business would be slow at work so that she could take a little longer break - maybe a lot of people would be busy outdoors sunbathing.

Once she got to BargainBin, she looked across the store immediately to see if any of the Collins family were working. She didn't see Tedwin, but Alith was there. *Hmm...he's late....or maybe he's in the freezer...I'll wait a while for my break.*

She hoped that he wasn't angry with her for not

thanking him for the doll - or for mumbling a goodbye and quickly getting out of the car like she was angry - she *was angry,* but only at herself for letting her emotions get the best of her.

Considering all that Tedwin had confided in her about himself and his family, she was worried that he was avoiding her and didn't want to see her again.

Thankfully business was slow, so Jessica said she could take a little longer break.

Alith knew Ella planned to come over and see where they worked, and Tedwin knew as well - but he was glad to be hiding in the freezer.

"It might freak her out to see us standing there - watching her, waiting for her," Tedwin advised his sister hours beforehand. "I'll work on organizing the walk-in freezer until you come get me."

Alith agreed with his plan, and also wanted just a few moments to talk to Ella - just the two of them - without Tedwin acting like she was embarrassing him. He didn't quite believe Alith and Ella would be best friends, even though he too had seen the visions - and the one that she shared with him now was Ella worrying about the awkward way they parted last time and not thanking him for the doll.

He didn't think it was as big of a deal as Ella was making it out to be, and he wasn't upset. "Can't you just tell her to thank me and get over it?" he inquired as politely as he could to his sister, using every ounce of influence he could muster - giving her a wide, inviting smile and pleading with his eyes - a combination he usually reserved for the school secretary when he needed to get excused from unexplained absences.

Alith playfully pretended to be shocked.

"No! Absolutely not! You saw how worried she is. She's over there pacing right now, trying to get the courage up to come over here." She poked him in the shoulder and raised her chin, adding, "and you need to apologize even if she doesn't, since you weren't at school today and she was hoping to talk to you. It might help her to know that she dazzled you too."

"Really?"

Alith gave him a naughty grin and then paused, her eyes momentarily changing focus as she saw something else. "Okay! She's decided! She's going to come over! Yay!"

Tedwin felt frozen - like a statue. He didn't say anything - or move - while Alith jumped up and gave him an eager hug. He hoped that he would be able to form coherent sentences and not get dazzled again in Ella's presence.

Finally - the moment came - when Alith saw the outline of Ella's frame begin to walk in their direction. Excitedly bouncing on the balls of her feet, she smiled at Ella as she got closer.

Ella felt excited, but still very shy as she approached. *Here goes. Don't be a coward, don't be a coward.*

She stopped at the counter to talk to Alith like any regular customer would.

"Hi...um, is Tedwin around?"

"Of course," Alith replied warmly. "By the way, you

and I are going to be great friends!" She cocked her head to the left. "He's in the freezer, I'll go get him. In fact, come on back, I'll unlock the side door for you." She motioned toward the left and disappeared before Ella could object.

Ella wasn't sure if she was allowed to be in a different store - kind of like how Wreck-It-Ralph wasn't supposed to be in anyone else's game.

Am I going Turbo? she thought as she went around to the side where there was a silver door that said in all capital letters EMPLOYEES ONLY. It opened with a creak and Alith stepped aside so she could come in.

The employee area was very nice and organized, more so than where Ella worked. The floor was covered with some kind of fancy marble tile, the stainless steel prep counters were also very large and expensive looking - not like the ones at Harrow Inn. The back wall was completely covered by a gigantic metal, walk-in freezer with a huge, heavy looking door.

Just these few things alone must have cost thousands of dollars in Ella's quick estimation.

Alith opened the large, freezer door with an ease that seemed odd for a girl of her small stature.

"Tedwin! Guess who came for a visit?"

Tedwin pretended to be a little surprised as he saw them, sliding a plastic bin back in place on one of the shelves, he came out, closing the door shut behind him.

"Ella," he greeted her politely, "So nice to see you. Thank you for coming by."

She glanced at the walk-in freezer for a few seconds, then back at him.

"Ah, your hang-out place?" she asked coyly.

Tedwin nodded and smiled, remembering he had told her about that when she commented on how cold his hand was before.

"I think it's time for my break. I'll give you a few minutes to look around," Alith said politely to the two of them. After a moment of silence she chidingly blurted out "*YOU'RE WELCOME!*" as neither of them said "thank you" - they just stood there staring at each other.

"I'm glad you came," Tedwin said kindly, "and I'm sorry for the way we said goodbye the other day. I meant to tell you I hoped to see you again, but I was just...well... my brain wasn't working." He hoped that would be a good enough explanation / apology and that she would accept it.

Ella was relieved that he wasn't angry at her and that he seemed to feel the same way about the incident. She was about to make a comment about how his eyes looked a different color of amber brown than the last time she had seen him, but she could feel herself starting to get caught off guard again, so she averted her eyes down to the floor.

"It's ok, my brain wasn't working either."

This was a good opportunity to change the subject, so she glanced around, still not looking at Tedwin or his eyes.

"Are you sure it's ok for me to be back here? Like, behind the counter? I mean, I'm not an employee, like the door says."

"Of course - Rose isn't here, so things are a little more... relaxed. Carlo and Escusme are around somewhere. You - however - *are* the first outsider. Come on, I'll show you around."

She followed Tedwin through the red, swinging door with a viewing window that separated the back of the store from the front.

The front of the store was very nice too: the same kind of expensive-looking, marble tile covered the floor in a diamond pattern, and the counter top appeared to be marble as well. The glass pendant lights that she had only been able to previously see from a distance, were also fancy, like they had been carefully handcrafted with swirls of red and orange colors dripped on them - not something you would find at the local hardware store.

Jackson was standing by the register next to Alith with his arms crossed, frowning at Ella's presence disapprovingly. Alith had told him they would be having a special visitor, but Jackson was not thrilled.

"You remember my boyfriend...erm...I mean, brother, Jackson? He's our newest *frigitarian*."

"Pleased to meet you, again." Jackson said with a smile that was really more of a way of talking through his teeth, his arms still crossed. Working in the same building as a pizza place was bad enough - but this girl was like a walking slice of deliciousness.

"Jackson hasn't been away from cooked food as long as the rest of us," Tedwin explained, "it's a little difficult for him sometimes."

Alith gracefully skipped over to him. "Walk with me," she said to him in a way that was more of a command than a request, taking his hands in hers and pulling him along with her. Passing in front of Ella and Tedwin on their way out, she gave Ella a wink, but Jackson stared straight ahead, ignoring them both.

"Pleasant, isn't he?" Tedwin said sarcastically, trying not to let Jackson ruin the mood. Tedwin went behind the wall for a moment and returned with a glittery baseball cap.

"Here," he said, fitting it on her head, the hat a little big for her small frame. "Now you look like you work here. If anyone comes over, just stand behind me."

Ella looked up at him from under the brim of the hat. She pressed her lips together in an uncomfortable way and looked down.

"What's wrong?"

"I don't look good in hats."

Hmm. Well, I could always make you.

Ella narrowed her eyes at him. "Make me what? Look good in hats? How are you going to do that? They always come down over the top of my ears, making me look like a little kid. You can't fix that."

Tedwin adjusted it so that brim came up a little and he could see her eyes - her big, beautiful, brown eyes. He didn't want to think about how cute she looked, so he focused on the next task he had planned.

"*SO*?" he asked, raising his eyebrows and rubbing his hands together. "What cold treat are you in the mood for?"

Rubbing his hands together didn't make his hands any warmer, but it was something he saw a lot on American TV when someone was plotting something.

"Oh!" Ella glanced sideways at the long counter. "Oh, that's a good question! I don't know, I don't even know what all you have."

"Okay, well I'll take you down the line of all of our flavors and you can pick. You can even have more than one, if you want."

There were 2 rows of ice creams down the length of the counter, separated into 2 sections. Each section was covered by a clear, plastic dome. The ice creams themselves were in metal, rectangular bins that had been inset so that just the top of the ice cream and the metal edge of the lip were visible.

Tedwin pulled the handle up on the first plastic dome to point out the flavors.

Along the bottom row were solid colors and the first one he pointed to was a peachy-red he called *Tiger's Blood*. The next, an orangy-red he called *Tarocco*, "which is Italian for blood orange", he explained, "we have little name tags on the customer side with English translations of the Italian words." The last one in the bottom row of the first section was a vibrant red he called *Bloody Mary*. "These along the top row are mixtures of the ones in the bottom row."

Ella marveled at how beautifully and intricately the colors in the top row had been swirled together, more beautiful than any Italian marble could hope to compare. The swirls of peaches, pinks and reds looked more like artwork than something to eat.

He closed the lid on the first dome and opened the second one. The solid color he pointed to next was a maroon color he called *Dark Cherry & Liver.*

Ella and Tedwin exchanged smiles, remembering that particular flavor as a snow cone Tedwin had brought her before.

The next one, an intense, brilliant red, he called *Red Velvet*. The next was *Frutti de Bosco,* a purplish red, which he explained was "Italian for mixed berries." He stopped and smiled as he introduced the last one on the bottom row: a deep, dark, chocolate.

"This is one of our Italian specialties, *Sanguinaccio Dolce*."

"Wow, that looks great!"

"Ella, come on, you said that about every flavor."

"Well, I thought they all looked pretty good."

"They are, but I'm not sure you want to try the Sanguinaccio today, it's an...*acquired* taste."

Pondering what he actually meant by that, she turned around, crossing her arms, and noticed a smaller dome on the counter behind them against the wall.

"What's that?"

As she looked down through the dome she could see that there were 4 bins filled with solid colors that looked different - like regular colors of ice cream.

"Oh, those. Those are our standard flavors down there - pistachio, lemon and peanut butter - and any of these can be used to make our *Sundae*

Bloody Sundae, including the other flavors. We just drizzle the top with chocolate and raspberry syrups, whipped cream and -

"You missed one."

Ella expected to see Alith when she turned around, but was surprised to see a short, young, blond-haired girl staring at them confidently. Ella looked up at Tedwin nervously and jumped a little bit when she saw Carlo and Escusme in her peripheral vision - she did not know where they had come from - or that they stood there silently giggling while watching her and Tedwin.

"*They are soo cute*," Escusme mouthed to Carlo just a few moments before Jade unlocked the side door and let herself in.

Tedwin was the first to speak.

"My apologies Jade. Ella, this one on the end is called *Vanill-Leah*, but nobody ever wants that one. Customers were asking for a plain, vanilla flavor, so we asked corporate to send us one," he explained patiently and respectfully, "but this particular vanilla has a very strong - (he tried to think of a way to explain it so that Ella would understand) - *wet dog* smell."

"Tedwin," Carlo gently corrected while smiling at Jade, "If corporate had known about the smell, they wouldn't have sent it to us. Isn't that right, Jade?"

"Of course," assured Jade in a slightly mocking tone. Ella thought she noticed her large eyes narrow a bit. "You should be getting a replacement shipment next week of our new and improved vanilla option, *Van-Emilly*."

"Well Jade, we certainly appreciate you coming all this way to tell us that - you are too kind," Carlo spoke again, in the same gentle manner. "May we offer you anything? Raspberry soda perhaps?"

Jade was not having any of his fake niceties.

"You're 8 days late with your quarterly financial statements. Aro sent me to see what was taking so long."

Carlo smiled at Jade again, endearingly - trying to lighten the mood. "Oh shoot!" he chuckled, "We had the UPS guy come pick them up at 10 this morning. If you had only arrived a few hours ago, you would have fulfilled your purpose."

"Pity...," Jade's tone was still dark, "It's not often I'm rendered useless."

The thick tension in the room was uncomfortable and strange.

She shifted her focus off of Carlo and locked in on Ella. Ella felt it too, as if suddenly she was in the cross-hairs of a rifle - defenseless and exposed.

"What's she doing here? She's not an employee."

"The girl is with us," Carlo replied, taking a few steps over to Ella and putting his arm around her and lightly resting his hand on her shoulder.

"She was just leaving. Tedwin, why don't you and Ella finish your break outside."

Tedwin and Ella took one step together when Jade's forceful bombardment of questions stopped Ella in her tracks.

"YOU - I want some answers. What are you *really*

doing back here? Who created glue? Do you talk in your sleep? Can more than 4 people play Candyland? What's 1.77245?" Can you smell what the Rock is cooking? Have you pooped your pants since Kindergarten? Is a hot dog a sandwich?

" Uh...," Ella stammered, "Yes, no, maybe...the square root of pi...um..." Ella's voice trailed off - Jade had asked her so many questions she forgot which questions she had asked first.

She looked around for help - where was Alith when she needed her most? She was so good at diffusing tense situations.

Tedwin had pressed his lips together, trying to hide a smile. *She doesn't know she talks in her sleep - how adorable.*

Everyone else's eyes were a little wide - even though they were trying to act normal - they couldn't hide the fact that they were all secretly wondering which question Ella had answered "maybe" to - as there were questions after "pi" that remained unanswered, and one involved the pooping of pants.

"She'll tell you anything you *need* to know," Escusme offered.

"I know," Jade replied smugly.

Escusme knew Ella was a bright girl - and Ella knew that no one needed to know about the sleepover birthday party she went to in the 9th grade. Her friend's dad made them breakfast burritos with a spicy, Mexican meat called *chorizo* (that her stomach apparently wasn't used to) on Saturday morning and then she and all her friends went to the mall - a very large mall, where signs for bathroom locations were unexpectedly challenging to find.

Carlo remembered her first question.

"We thought it would be a good idea to put a hat on her for a few minutes while we showed her around, in case any customers came."

Tedwin was relieved that this wasn't a lie, but he knew Jade wouldn't approve.

"That wasn't yours to offer."

"She didn't know what she was doing," Escusme interjected, "we'll take responsibility for her."

"Aro will be interested to know that you had a non-employee back here. Are you going to follow the rules? Or, are we going to have to send someone from corporate down here to keep an eye on you and make sure you get your statements to us on time? Decisions, decisions..."

"Ella will be one of us - I've seen it!" a voice cried out.

Alith and Jackson had sprinted in from their break, not bothering to come in the employee door, just stopping right in front of the store at the counter. She had not upheld the lighthearted tone that Carlo was trying so hard to keep during this potentially disastrous encounter.

A long 15 seconds passed while everyone waited for Jade's response, hoping no one sitting at the picnic tables in the middle of BargainBin had seen or heard the commotion.

Finally Jade spoke: "I doubt that. Just remember,

corporate doesn't give second chances." She abruptly turned and exited. When the employee door clicked shut behind her, everyone breathed a sigh of relief.

CHAPTER 11: THE MIRACLE

The mood was still tense - everyone was motionless, standing still as statues.

"Well then...we still have a break we need to take." Tedwin offered as he studied Ella's emotionless face, trying to figure out how she was feeling - hoping she would stay.

"Yeah, we do." Ella didn't seem too shaken up about what had just happened.

Tedwin was impressed.

"So did you decide what flavor you want?"

"Um...I don't know...like, give me some time, maybe." Ella paused and bit her lip, looking over the rows of flavors. "How about...how about you just give me a scoop of each one of the solid flavors? Except for the smelly vanilla and the special Italian chocolate one you pointed out."

"Okay, I think we can do that."

"Are you sure you don't want to try the *Vanill-Leah*?"

"No, I believe you. I mean, I don't know how you can really mess up vanilla ice cream though. Isn't all vanilla the same?"

"Well, you would *think*", he explained, excited to share some of the more scientific properties of their products that he had been studying in his free time, "but there are small differences in the chemical compounds from each plant that affect how it tastes to varying degrees. It's not *actually* the taste that's the problem, technically, as sugar covers up most of it - but the *stench*, however - is revolting." He shrugged. "I guess it's just the way our family's olfactory senses were trained as far as that goes...but for some reason, we all agree that most vanilla extracts, and especially this one in particular - smells *exactly like wet dog* - it's weird."

"When you say...'we'" -

"I mean my family and myself" he snapped quickly. "But," he added a little more gently, "I would be interested to know what you think about it, how it smells to you. Feel like giving it a sniff?"

Ella thought for a minute. "I guess I've probably baked with it before, but don't remember ever smelling it - and... I don't think I want to, it sounds gross."

"Hmm...I could always make you." Tedwin smiled at the idea - even though he was technically almost a grown man, he still liked making girls smell things that were icky or gross, especially Rose - she was his favorite to mess with.

Last week when she was being particularly - *Rose-ish* - he had put her in a headlock and made her smell a sock he had found out in the woods. He often found random pieces of clothing out there, usually jean shorts and athletic shoes - it was very odd.

"I'm pretty sure you can't make me do anything," she commented wryly. "How about you just ask me? I'm not afraid."

He opened a cabinet above them and took out a dark, skinny, glass jar. He looked over his shoulder at Ella and grinned, "*Eau de woof*, coming up," he said as he turned back to the jar and unscrewed the lid a little.

Turning around and removing the lid all the way, he inhaled the faint aroma of the scent himself - his face a good six inches away - ah *yes, still revolting*. Holding the jar in his right hand he moved it in her direction a little and cautioned her:

"All right, take a whiff - but keep your distance, it's pretty strong."

Taking a small step closer to Tedwin and leaning forward a bit, she inhaled gently - and immediately her eyebrows shot up in a surprised expression.

"Wow, I can see what you've been talking about! It really does stink!"

"WHAT IS THAT AWFUL WET DOG SMELL!!!" a voice yelled from behind the door. It was Alith - peering through the viewing window, trying to see what was going on, her nose turned up and pressed against the glass, making her look like a little piggy.

Tedwin had better not be making her smell that vanilla extract...if he is, why couldn't I see him doing that? She pushed the door open and in a flash was next to her brother.

"TEDWIN MASEN COLLINS!" she exclaimed while glaring at him, her mouth open in surprise. "Are you making her *smell* that?"

Before giving Tedwin a moment to answer she swiftly stepped in between him and Ella.

"Is he making you smell that? Cause if he is he's in BIG trouble. He's supposed to be being *nice* to you. Ella's been through enough today!"

She turned and slapped Tedwin on the arm and gave him a serious look that only a mom gives a child when they are acting up in public. She didn't want Tedwin scaring off her potential best friend and ruining all of their futures - especially after the scare Jade had given them.

"*Oww-ha-howww,*" Tedwin laughed as he feigned hurt and held his arm like her slap had actually caused him pain. Deep down he knew the only thing that could ever actually hurt him was Ella - and he didn't know how long he could actually keep that a secret from her.

"No, he didn't make me do anything." Ella cleared her throat and put her shoulders back a little. "I'm a strong, independent woman. Besides, if I *choose* to smell it, it has nothing to do with you."

Alith sighed. "Why don't you two pick out your snacks and take it over there where you can't get into trouble," she said as looked in the direction of the picnic tables then back at Tedwin. "Jackson and I will take over while you eat."

Tedwin finished scooping all of the flavors she requested into the largest bowl they had - even their largest bowl had left a few of the scoops extending over the edge a bit - which he hoped wouldn't drip.

Ella saw what Tedwin had made her and smiled as she remembered something funny.

"I saw this movie once where they would bring out a big bowl of ice cream with a scoop of everything and if you finished it all, they would come out and put a pig sticker on your shirt and chant *"ziggy piggy"* and blow a horn and make oinking noises at you. You're not going to do that, are you?" Ella asked very concernedly.

"No, don't worry," Tedwin reassured her while chuckling, "I don't think you'll even be able to finish half of that bowl."

He scooped himself the darker chocolate, the Italian flavor, into a cone - and topped it with a slice of blood orange. Grabbing a pink spoon from the silverware canister, he carefully stuck one in the top of Ella's bowl.

They chose an empty table farthest away from where anyone else was sitting, there was only one other table occupied on this slow evening.

Ella tried the mixed berry scoop first. *Soo good!*

"Wow, this i*s amazing!*" she mused out loud. Glancing down at her bowl, she furrowed her eyebrows in surprise and amazement. "I know I have 10 more flavors to try...but honestly, I can't imagine it gets any better than this!"

Tedwin was pleased, but smiled and said nothing.

Ella was curious as to how such an amazing tasting ice cream existed in her tiny little town. "So how did you and your family get into the ice cream business? I mean it seems a lot different from..." Ella chose her words carefully, not wanting to mention anything Tedwin had warned her about. "From what you *used* to do."

"Well this story is a neat one, actually. When we lived in Santa Clara, we found this Italian gelato shop that really reminded us of home. Their *sanguinaccio dolce* was to die for."

He looked at Ella - sitting across from him, listening intently to his words. Keeping their past a secret was of utmost importance, but when it came to Ella, he wanted her to know him, and that included everything he had been through.

The words seemed to pour out of him with ease despite his reservations. "It's an old Italian recipe for a chocolate pudding-like dessert that uses animal blood instead of eggs, which makes it easy to turn into a gelato."

"Are you for real?" Ella asked, she had never heard of using anything like that in a recipe.

"Yes, I know it probably sounds gross to you, but blood actually has similar fat and protein ratios to eggs - you can google it. Carlo told me when he was a boy they would make it every winter when the people in the village would gather together to slaughter their pigs in the town square - it was kind of like a festival. Instead of wasting the blood - they didn't want to waste any part of the animal, so they would collect the blood while it was still fresh and before it had coagulated. Then they would add chocolate and sugar to it, and give it to all the children as a special treat."

Ella didn't say anything. She rubbed the back of her neck with her hand. Tedwin couldn't tell how uncomfortable she was, her face was serious but didn't give him any clues otherwise. He decided to continue with his story.

"Anyways, Escusme struck up a friendship with the owners of the gelato shop and they said they were interested in making the business into a franchise, so when we decided to move up here, we became their first franchisees. Escusme says we have too much time on our hands anyways, she wants us to be productive and learn something useful in our free time. *"You live in the land of opportunity - don't waste it"* - she always tells us. So I guess in a way, it's similar to some of the things we did before - but now we only deal in the blood of animals, during the one or two times out of year we make it - and we get it legally from Mr. Ross, the butcher. We use it to bring people happiness."

"Is the sanguacho..." Ella knew she was butchering the name. "Is that the only flavor that has actual blood in it?"

"Yeah, I think so. Most of the flavors right now are shipped here from corporate, except for that one we make ourselves. We are getting a larger gelato machine soon that will allow us to make all of them right here."

Tedwin looked up and frowned. He saw Jason Dark-Gray walking in the direction of Harrow Inn, looking for Ella.

"*Oooh...nice biceps,*" he heard Jess think as she slowly sauntered toward the counter to see if this super buff cutie wanted to order something. She knew she should walk quicker since business had been really slow that evening, but she wanted more time to ogle him.

Tedwin read Jason's mind too, and could see that he was excited to ask Ella if she still wanted to go cliff diving on Sunday, weather permitting. Neither of those words sounded safe: when it came to Ella, either of those two words could be dangerously life-threatening.

Tedwin didn't know how he would stop them. *Maybe I can stop him now, make him turn around, make something up. Yes, that's right, we happen to be on a date, and she doesn't want him around.*

Tedwin checked to see if Ella was looking in Jason's direction or if she was still focused on her bowl of ice cream.

"If I asked you to stay here and eat your ice cream while I took care of something, would you?" Tedwin asked, annoyed at Jason's interruption.

Always in the way.

Ella had noticed his eyes following someone, so she turned around to see who it was.

"Of course not," Tedwin muttered disappointedly with a half smile.

"*Jason! Jason is here!*" she exclaimed excitedly and stood up, waving at him with both arms overhead, not aware that he might have been the person

Tedwin was watching.

"Jaaason! Come over here!" She called out to him, waving hello as he saw and recognized her. She sat back down on the side of her chair and waited for him.

Turning to face Tedwin once he arrived, she introduced them.

"Jason, this is Tedwin, he got me this ice cream and I'm going to eat *ALL* of it. Tedwin, this is my friend Jason. We used to make mud pies together."

"Speak for yourself. I made two just this morning," he replied seriously. Ella would have never guessed that this was something he hadn't outgrown - but he loved it.

"We've met," stated Tedwin coldly, his eyes flashing momentarily with an emotion that Ella could not decipher.

Jason stared down at the huge bowl of ice cream in front of Ella, his mouth falling open in shock and disbelief.

"You're going to make her eat that???" he asked incredulously.

"No," Ella responded, "he can't make me do anything, we've established that."

Jase leaned down closer to her face. "What are you thinkin' Ella?"

Ella drew back, confused by his behavior, but she laughed and smiled. It did look like a *lot* of food - but Ella was confident in her ability to eat much more than people expected her to. And, she didn't know why Jason seemed to care so much. It was just ice cream. And she was a teenager.

"Look, I can do this Jase, I'm strong enough."

Jason snorted sarcastically. "You can spout that stuff to your...*whatever* over there," his eyes narrowing as he focused on Tedwin, hoping this wasn't her new boyfriend, "but you can't fool me."

He shook his head as he walked a few steps away. He paused for a moment, looking up, scrunching the hair on the back of his head in his fists like he always did when he was frustrated. He then turned and walked back to Ella and leaned down, gently putting his hand around her own.

She had taken a momentary break from eating as she watched his overblown reaction to this completely normal situation and was resting her wrist on the edge of the table, spoon facing up, and wasn't super thrilled that now his hand was almost touching her spoon. Him leaning down was making her freak out a little too, she didn't want him breathing germs on her spoon either.

Just...*don't do this*," he pleaded with his best puppy dog eyes.

"Look, I know you think that for some reason this is a scary thing, but it's not," she reassured him, giving him a sympathetic look. He was overreacting - big time. "I can scarf whatever I want: pizza, pizza flavored Doritos, pizza rolls, pizza pockets... and I don't gain any weight!"

Ella looked down and put her hand lovingly against her mostly flat stomach: palm first, then fingers. "It's like this miracle or something." Her face broke into a radiant, tender smile - her face: beaming, her skin: glowing.

"Ha! Well, wait until you turn 30," Jason retorted. "You can only have high blood sugar for so long before it starts to damage your circulation... or even kills you."

Jason was not speaking theoretically. The memories of how his mother kept their freezer and pantry full of junk food like ice cream, frozen pizzas, chips, cookies and burritos - was all too vivid.

He had tried to sneak in a bag of frozen vegetables a few times, but she always found them and threw them in the trash.

She had passed away nearly 3 years before from uncontrolled diabetes and he watched as she suffered painful and life-altering amputations: first it was just a few toes, then it was her feet, and finally her legs.

He had imagined the sugar spreading throughout her body like poison, a venom. Destroying every tissue, organ and nerve it touched - at least that's how his 13 year old mind pictured it. The doctors said that it was her heart that gave out in the end - and he was powerless to stop it. But now, there was absolutely *no way* he could let this happen to anyone else he cared about.

"Just promise me you'll cut back on the carbs, eat a salad every now and then, ok? I know you love pizza and ice cream and junk, but sometimes...sometimes you've gotta learn to love what's *good for you*. I don't want you to end up like my mom."

"Hey," she pulled her hand back, removing it from his, and stuck her spoon back into her bowl. "I'm as healthy as a horse. And I do eat salad...sometimes."

Jason howled with laughter - if only Ella had known what she had just said.

"No - I'M AS HEALTHY AS A HORSE!" he managed to vocalize once he caught his breath.

Tedwin and Ella waited for him to provide an explanation as to what had him so amused - but he did not oblige.

He looked at Tedwin disgustedly. "If she gets sick, it's on you. She might need her toes someday."

Of course Tedwin had considered the consequences of his culinary choices, but he could only take so much of Jason's odor - the barnyard smell he remembered from Ella's house, radiating off him - just like his heat. He cleared his throat and exhaled to try to prevent the smell from taking a foothold.

"I need some hydration," Tedwin stated as he stood up, "Ella, would you care for a bottle of water?"

"I could care less what you need," Jason interrupted, standing face to face with Tedwin.

"Feeling dehydrated? Maybe you need to go to the hospital," he barked, his chest puffed out, his eyes angry. "Do you want me to *put* you in the hospital?"

"I'll get you one anyways," Tedwin replied dismissively, ignoring Jason's threats. "She doesn't need you telling her what to do."

Jason lunged after him and grabbed his arm as he attempted to walk away. "You don't speak for her!"

Tedwin shook his hand off, now he was angry. He turned around, using his few inches of height over Jason to stare him down.

Completely confused again by Jason's behavior, Ella jumped to her feet and grabbed Jason's arm, pulling him away a little from Tedwin.

"What's your problem?" she exclaimed.

Ella glanced down at her hand, burning as it rested on his tan skin. She drew back her hand quickly, and the heat subsided. She put it back again and couldn't believe what she was feeling. *Oh, ok, if this intensity has to do with losing his mom...then that does make sense*.

"Wow, Jase, you're like...*hot*...are you okay? Do you have a fever?"

"I have to go," he digressed, his anger melting into what it really was: sadness.

He could see that for now, she was not going to make healthy choices - she was going to sit there with Tedwin and finish her huge bowl of ice cream - but he had done what he could.

He was less angry as he spoke, his sadness becoming apparent in his voice. "I can see what that stuff is doing to you. It's a killer, Ella." He took a few steps back from their table. "I know how this ends, and I'm not st-..." He tried to think of a word to replace *sticking* - but staying also started with the same letters. He couldn't disobey Sam - no matter where he was. "I'm not...hanging around to watch," were his final words to Ella.

She didn't understand why he suddenly had to

go. She watched him leap over a picnic table as he dashed toward the exit, losing sight of him as a tall pile of jeans was being wheeled in.

"Jason," she murmured to herself, tears unexpectedly filling her eyes, wondering if she would ever see him again. She stood there for a few moments, stunned by his strange behavior, twirling a strand of her hair.

She knew where she had to go to see him again: she would have to go to the reservation.

When she finally turned around, Tedwin was holding two water bottles. *How did he get those so fast?*

They both sat back down silently, staring at the bowl of ice cream that still had 3 scoops left.

"Thanks for the water."

With her palate now cleansed from a few gulps of fresh, cold water - Ella was determined to finish her bowl of ice cream.

"You know, I was remembering something while you were showing me the ice cream flavors earlier. I remember one time at camp I ate a -"

"CAMP??? YOU???" Tedwin laughed heartily. "Sorry, I just couldn't help laughing at the mental picture of you doing anything outdoorsy, like going to camp."

Well, I only went the one year. We stayed in cabins. I didn't find it particularly enjoyable. But what I was *going to say before you so rudely interrupted,* is that one day we hiked about an hour to this waterfall, and someone gave me a cherry flavored Starburst and when I bit down on it with my back teeth, one of my loose molars got stuck in it, and I took it out of my mouth and my tooth was in it."

"What did you do after that?"

"I took my tooth out of it and put the tooth in my pocket. The Starburst was still good, so I ate it. My gum was bleeding where the tooth was, and it mixed with the flavor of the candy - and it wasn't *"terrible"* - I just wasn't used to the taste of blood. The cherry and liver snow cone you made me the other day tasted a little familiar, but I wasn't able to put my finger on where I had tasted it before until I saw the ice cream made with blood y'all have and I remembered camp."

"That's...interesting. I'm glad you survived."

"Well, I almost didn't, I had a few close calls."

Of course she had some close calls. "Okay let's hear them," Tedwin said amusedly.

"At the waterfalls, I slipped and fell on a rock that had moss on it and banged my shin really hard. It didn't bleed but it swelled up and I had a big goose egg on top and I could barely walk for 2 days. That wasn't fun. Also, on the way to the waterfalls, we stopped and sat for a while where there were some benches and logs. I sat on a log and there was a log across from mine that a lot of people were sitting on, and I noticed a snake underneath it. I yelled for the counselors and they moved everyone away and identified it as a baby timber rattlesnake - the babies are more dangerous than the adults because they're at their most uncontrollable when it comes to how much venom they inject when they bite."

"Were you afraid?"

"No."

"Really?"

"Yeah, really. It was beautiful. It stayed under the log while we all moved to another location. I wish I could have gotten a picture or something."

Tedwin only had a moment to marvel at her bravery - the bravery of this frail looking girl - before his mind was interrupted.

Ella noticed that he looked away for a moment, his eyes becoming distant.

"Alith just had a vision of you standing on a cliff. Don't you think that seems...*dangerous* for someone like you?"

"Oh. She's good! Yeah, Jase and I were supposed to go...cliff jumping, near the reservation this weekend."

"Why would you do something like that?" he asked astonishedly, trying not to sound angry. "Are you trying to get yourself killed?"

"No, silly, it's just recreationally. Jase and his friends do it all the time, I've watched them."

Tedwin knew he couldn't keep her from going, and not just anyone was welcome on Paiute lands.

"Okay, well if you do go - can you promise me one thing?"

"Maybe. What's that?"

"I don't want to offend you, but try not to do anything dangerous - for Charlie's sake. Falling in the ocean doesn't sound like such a good idea for someone like you. We both know you have a tendency to be... clumsy - so can you just be a spectator and not a participant?"

"Jason doesn't get to tell me what to do - and neither do you."

Ella put the last spoonful of ice cream in her mouth and dropped the spoon from about a foot above it, the plastic bouncing against the porcelain bowl as it landed.

"DONE," she said satisfactorily. She had eaten the entire bowl and was completely fine.

"Here's your hat back," she said in an irritated tone, placing the hat on the table and sliding it in Tedwin's direction. "My break time is over. See you later."

Tedwin wasn't overly pleased about how today's interaction with Ella was ending, but he respected her for standing up to him - and to Jason.

Ella wasn't particularly happy either, but this was her life - and no one was going to tell her how to live it. If Tedwin - or Jason - wanted to be a part of her life, they would have to accept her choices.

CHAPTER 12: THE SHORT LIFE OF MR. FLUFFKINS

Ella wasn't sure about going to the reservation unannounced, but this was the weekend she and Jason had previously decided to go cliff diving.

Even though he ran off last time she saw him, maybe she would call him just one more time to see if he still wanted to go. He hadn't been answering his phone - he probably needed some time to think or cool off.

Charlie had left early that morning to go fishing and cell service wasn't too good where he was, so she couldn't ask him about protocols.

It was fine though, she didn't really want to talk about boy problems with her dad anyhow, although he had told her that Jason had asked to come over while she was at school last week and hadn't said anything else.

Billy finally picked up the phone.

"Hi Mr. Dark-Gray, this is Ella. Is Jase home?"

"Hi Ella, yeah - I think he's out in the shed, I'll go get him, just a minute."

Billy knew that Jason was avoiding her phone calls, but he was tired of not answering the phone when it rang.

Ella could hear Billy yelling at him that Ella was on the phone for him - everyone within a half-mile radius could probably hear too.

"Ella, hey Loca - what's up?" Jason tried to act nonchalant as he finally answered her call, but Ella wasn't having any of it.

"Hey!!! Why haven't you called me back??? I was worried about you!"

"Oh, sorry - yeah I meant to, I was just...sorry, sometimes guys are dumb. So, you doing ok?"

His apology softened her anger. "Yeah, I'm ok - but my dad said you asked to come over while I was gone - what's that about? I mean, you don't want to see me?"

"Yeah, I hope you're not upset about that. Your dad told my dad that you were having nightmares. I called Charlie, and he said I could go upstairs and take a look around at the decor in your room while you were out."

That was weird. "Why would you need to look at my room?"

"Well, I know a guy who makes some things to help people sleep, and I wanted it to match your style. I wanted the whole thing to be a surprise, but... I guess you seeing it will be the surprise. So, you still hanging out with... *that guy*?" he asked, not able to hide the irritation in his voice

"Well, for your information, A: I'm not a big fan of surprises. And B: not that it's really any of your business, but yes," Ella replied, not hiding the irritation in her own voice, either.

"Tedwin is in my life now."

Jason said nothing.

She took a breath and asked him something else she had been wondering about.

"By the way, I was going to ask you...right after I started work, I went out for some fresh air behind the store and I lost my ring somewhere on the trail, and when I went back to go look for it, a guy came out of the woods and said he saw some strange animals in there. Do you know anything about that? Were they some of yours"

"Uhhh..." There was more silence.

"Jason? Are you there?"

"Yeah, I'm still here." He tried to think of a way to explain without revealing anything more than what she needed to know.

"Well - a few of our animals did get out recently. They must have come in contact with someone, because one of them had a human snack." This was a great reply - and he was very proud of himself. This was also the explanation he gave to Sam for not keeping up with the rest of the herd that day they were chasing after the strange animal.

The words hit Ella in a different way - fear gripped her heart. *Oh no! That poor guy went back into the woods... and they ate him!* She wasn't sure how to proceed with the conversation. She didn't want him to know that she knew. *He said it so nonchalantly... how could he?* Jason was a good kid, maybe she could convince him that their loose animals eating people wasn't okay - it was wrong.

" Look Jase...I just want you to know, whatever's going on, it's not normal. But I'm here for you."

Jason's tone suddenly turned dark and defensive. "Ok then, speaking of 'normal behavior', what's with the filthy bloodsucker in your bed?"

"I... I don't know what you're talking about," Ella stammered.

"You know *exactly* what I'm talking about. You can lie to everyone else, but you can't fool me - I've seen it."

Ella waited for Jase to say something else to explain. The silence was killing her.

"Your vampire doll!" he finally exclaimed as he laughed heartily - he was just joking, but he gave her quite a scare.

"Sheesh, Jason! Don't scare me like that!" *Ah, yes - The Count.* Ella had forgotten that she kept it next to her pillow.

"Tedwin gave him to me to help me sleep. He has quite a collection of stuffed animals."

"Tedwin has 'stuffed' animals? Wow...that's just so...it's so *wrong*. You really shouldn't be hanging around with someone like that, Ella."

Now it was Ella's turn to laugh heartily. He had some nerve telling her what was right and wrong.

"Like what, Jason? What's wrong with having stuffed animals?"

"It makes me sick Ella - they're not even *alive*," he spat. "You need something real - with flesh and blood - and *warmth*."

Ella couldn't believe the conversation they were having. "Of course they're not *alive*, Jason - they're just pretend," she reassured him, "calm down." She understood his love of animals, of protecting them, but he wasn't understanding.

She didn't think animal heads were tasteful home decor either, but that was another subject.

"You need to hear the truth Ella - they used to be walking around, living peacefully, and now they'll always be like this: stiff, frozen - never moving forward with their lives."

Ella shook her head and smacked her hand against her forehead. She could see how he misunderstood what she was talking about.

"They aren't REAL - Jason - and they NEVER WERE. I'm not talking about taxdermied animals. I'm talking about toys, they're JUST toys. And besides....I don't want another real animal...not after Mr. Fluffkins."

Jacob was about to acquiesce to the fact that he understood she was just talking about toys - even though he was a bit embarrassed to admit it - but when she said "*Mr. Fluffkins*", it caught him off guard and bellowed again with laughter.

"Mr... *Who*?"

Ella held the phone by her side as she walked across

the room, not listening to Jason still howling with laughter - debating whether or not to talk about her precious pet - feeling hurt that he had laughed, even though it wasn't his fault that he didn't know.

She exhaled and held the phone up to her face again.

"It's not funny...Mr. Fluffkins was my pet chinchilla. I used to sleep with him in my bed, he was so cute! And I loved him so much. But one night... one night... I rolled over and squished him. I've never forgiven myself."

She took a deep breath, she *had* to address the bigger issue in her mind.

"Besides, you have a lot of nerve telling me it's wrong to kill animals... when your animals are out there in the woods killing human beings."

There was more silence.

"We're not killing people, Ella. We're just trying to protect them from..." his voice trailed off. "Hey, I've gotta go, Sam's here." Jason's tone had suddenly turned serious and curt.

"You've...gotta go," said Ella disappointedly. Having phone conversations - or even real life conversations - was always difficult with Jase. There was always some kind of drama or misunderstanding - and that's just how it was. But she was also disappointed that she hadn't had a chance to discuss if he still wanted to go cliff jumping.

"Can I come visit you later...or tomorrow?"

"Uh, I don't think that's such a good idea." He still hadn't decided if it was possible to be friends with

Ella, in spite of her self-destructive ways. Sam was helping him work through his feelings.

"I need some time. Don't call me, I'll call you."

"Really? 'Don't call me, I'll call you?'"

There was only silence now.

"Jase? Hello...? Are you there? Wow...I can't believe he actually hung up on me."

She sat on the foot of her bed for what seemed like a long time, trying to figure out what to do, before she finally decided to take a shower, go to bed early, and sleep on it. It was in her dreams that decided to go see Jason the next day, whether he wanted to see her or not.

Charlie heard her taking a shower, but as usual, wasn't sure if this wasn't some ploy to sneak out later.

After disconnecting her engine cables, he came back inside before she was done. Watching baseball for another few hours, just to make sure she stayed inside, he fell asleep on the couch.

At 2:30 A.M., while Ella was deep in sleep and making unconscious decisions, Alith's mind - not in any kind of sleep state - was invaded with a vision of Ella getting in her truck to go to the reservation. In a matter of seconds, Tedwin was on his way to disable Ella's truck - but Alith stopped him at the front door.

"Don't bother, Charlie already beat you to it."

In his hurry, he hadn't bothered to notice how the vision ended.

"Impressive!" Tedwin remarked, seeing the scene in her mind of a frustrated Ella, unable to start her truck.

Alith nodded in agreement. She was glad that Charlie had done it - not so much for Ella's safety, but because she wanted Tedwin to play the piano for her. It had been so long since he had filled the house with music, as he was spending way too much of his time watching Ella's house while she slept.

Tedwin smiled to himself and opened a can of V8, amused that he and Charlie had the same thoughts of sabotage when it came to keeping Ella safe.

"I'm liking chief Schwann a little more now," he said, taking a big gulp of the salty, red liquid.

He let his hand drop from the bronze door latch and put it around Alith's shoulder as they walked back inside toward the piano room.

Ella tried to start the truck around noon the next day, to no avail. She came back inside to the kitchen table, where Charlie was casually cleaning his rifles.

"Hey Dad, the truck won't start. I need to go see Jason today."

"Oh, Jason? Good," he said cheerfully, "I was hoping you would get to spend some time with him." He set his gun down on the table, next to his plate with a half-eaten sandwich on it, and stood up. "I'll go check under the hood," he said innocently, "see if there's anything noticeable."

With the fuel injectors plugged securely back in, Charlie started up the truck and slid out of the driver's seat so Ella could get in.

Although Charlie and Tedwin both approved of

sabotage, their reasons for reversing it were quite different - and unlike Ella - Charlie's decisions were not being watched.

"Seems fine now. Tell Billy hi for me," he said, peeking around the hood of the truck before slamming it shut and pulling up on it a bit to make sure it was secure.

Stepping back, he waved goodbye as Ella headed toward the reservation - determined to go cliff jumping, whether Jason joined her or not - a decision that would change the world she thought she lived in forever.

Find out what happens next to Ella, Tedwin and Jason
 in *The Ovenlight Saga: Baking Dough - Part 2*
 p.s. If you thought part 1 was bad - part 2 is worse! Here are
 the questions you will find answers to:

Who is eating magic monster muffins and why?
What does Ella get for Valentines Day?
What really happened to that field of purple flowers?
Why is Ella's life in danger?

EPILOGUE

First of all, thank you for purchasing my book. I know you could have picked any number of books to read, but you picked this one, and for that I am extremely grateful!

Whatever you think about this book, I'd like to hear from you. Your feedback and support will help me greatly improve my writing craft!

So to all of you wonderful readers, please be so kind as to leave a review of my book at the site you purchased it from. Your review is very important! Thank you so much for reading!

p.s. If you *REALLY REALLY ENJOYED MY BOOK* I would also be very appreciative if you could share it with your friends and family by posting to your social media accounts (Facebook, Instagram and Twitter, etc.)

Follow "The Ovenlight Saga" for updates on the release of Baking Dough: Part 2 (and also for funny Twilight memes)

Facebook: https://www.facebook.com ovenlightsaga

Instagram: https://www.instagram.com/ovenlightsaga/

Linktree & Website: https://linktr.ee/ovenlightsaga

ACKNOWLEDGMENTS

There are some other people that I need to acknowledge for making all of this possible.

My favorite funny movies and TV shows for making me laugh over and over again: *Encino Man, The Sasquatch Gang, The Goldbergs, Studio C, Brooklyn 9-9, The Office, Parks & Recreation, Jack & Jill, Home Alone, Saturday Night Live, The Wedding Singer, Sidekicks* (with Chuck Norris), *Office Space, Shanghai Noon, Zoolander 1 & 2, Shaun of the Dead, The Mask, The Benchwarmers, Monty Python & the Holy Grail, Bill & Ted's Excellent Adventure,* and *Spaceghost Coast to Coast* (the one with Brak). I would also like to give a shoutout to Weird Al Yankovic and Mel Brooks for making some great parodies and inspiring me with their work.

Winona Ryder for playing the part of Jo March so amazingly in "Little Women": thank you for the example and inspiration to be a writer - and to Mrs. Yvette Sharp for encouragement.

Blood donors: you saved my life! I got 2 units of blood at Memorial Hermann Hospital in The Woodlands when I experienced an episode of uncontrollable bleeding due to undiagnosed endometrial cancer. I had 2 great nurses, Debhe and Kayla, they were so loving & kind to me during a very scary time. Thank you.

The doctors and nurses at LBJ Hospital and MD Anderson in Houston (May - October 2021, Dr. Ruah-Hain Fernandez, Dr. Shaffer and many others), thank you for doing the surgery, chemo and radiation.

All those in the Twilight facebook groups: thank you for making hilarious Twilight memes and for providing a place so I could share my own. You made me laugh and gave me a place to be visually creative when I felt like I was *literally* hanging on to life by a thread after cancer treatments. Thanks to the admins who approved my posts.

Those who served in our military and gave their lives so I could have this freedom, to live in the greatest country in the world, to have the freedom of speech, to write and make memes and be creative without the threat of jail time or worse -thank you.

The millions of people who didn't get to be born or to live, to experience basic human rights and to pursue their ideas, interests or dreams because of the color of their skin, religion or gender, or because they lived under or are currently under oppressive dictatorships or murderous communist or socialist political regimes, I am mindful of you as I take this opportunity to pursue my own dreams. Even as silly as this is, writing a book feels like something everyone should have the opportunity to do. (My real dream btw is for this to get turned into a movie, like how *Spaceballs* was a parody of *Star Wars*, but with no bad stuff in it. That would be awesome!)

ABOUT THE AUTHOR

Stefanie Mellor

Stefanie Mellor grew up in the dry, desert plains of west Texas in the Midland/Odessa area and for the last few years has lived in the piney, coastal woods near Houston, Texas, where she enjoys being an aunt to 3 fantastic kids. She never enjoyed English class, or pictured herself EVER writing fiction, so this is a surprising endeavor - but one she has thoroughly enjoyed! She also believes – as Edward does – in saving sexual intimacy for marriage.

P.s. If you're wondering if I'm team Edward or team Jacob - I'm neither. Edward is not attractive to me, I don't think he's cute, he thinks he knows what's best for Bella and walks around hating himself all the time. Jacob also thinks he knows what's best for Bella, I mean his theory makes more sense, but you can't force it. Charlie, who's her dad and should know just a little bit about what *might* be best for Bella, thinks it's best to send her off to Jacksonville to live with her mom instead of sending her to therapy! So I'm not going to choose who or what is best for Bella - ONLY SHE can do that - but the girl definitely needs therapy to deal with her abandonment issues before embarking on any kind of romantic relationship. Just my 2 cents.

Made in United States
Troutdale, OR
05/28/2024